Irish Spy Agency (ISA) Chronicles
Book 2: Chain Retrieval

By Damien Murphy

Copyright © 2023 Damien Murphy
All rights reserved.
ISBN: 9798376146385

'If Your Presence isn't with me,
I don't wanna Move.
If Your Spirit's not what guides me,
Bring me back to You.'

Mason Kerby (2023) Beltway Park Church Abilene Texas

There is no point in moving forward in your life without God.
Life with God is the biggest adventure you will ever go on in life.

Dedication

To my nieces and nephew,

May your all hopes and dreams come true.

Contents

Preface

Chapter 1: The Trip

Chapter 2: The Map

Chapter 3: Mariana Trench

Chapter 4: The History of the ISA

Chapter 5: Irish Spy Agency Official Training

Chapter 6: My Team

Chapter 7: The Sistine Chapel, Italy

Chapter 8: Rebekah Clark

Chapter 9: Jacob's Ladder, Texas

Chapter 10: Hippodrome Aeon Circus, Galway & Hookhead Lighthouse, Wexford

Chapter 11: Carabalk Isle

Preface

With only one chain left to get before we bring Daniel home, we flew off towards the Island floating in the air.
The island was beautiful but unfortunately it didn't last long that way because Daniel and he goons arrived and attacked us. They need all the chains to get rid of us but we would never let that happen.
My plan is going to work and we will get Daniel home and we take down the goons and their boss before they destroy the entire world.
We put my plan into action and Daniel was fighting against us one moment and after we did a little magic if you will, Daniel was back on our side.

Irish Spy Agency (ISA) Chronicles Book 2: Chain Retrieval

With Daniel's help we made the island beautiful again. Daniel filled us in on a lot of what happened to him when he was with the goons.

The news shocked us all to our core including Paul.

Chapter 1: The Trip

My mother had worked as doctor her entire life, and hardly as anytime off, so we never travelled outside Ireland. "This is going to be so much fun," I screamed, "I'm going to be taking pictures everywhere we go." They all laughed at me.

"Where are we off to, Paul?" Peter and Molly asked. "I found the first chain," Paul stated as we waited in anticipation , "I found it in Australia. Now for you to get these chains you will have to focus and hone in on your powers, just like Daniel thought you.

"You gotta use your jetpacks to get around the world. People know who you are now so we gotta do this silently, don't cause a scene to draw attention."

Irish Spy Agency (ISA) Chronicles Book 2: Chain Retrieval

"Paul, it was Daniel who got us to fight at the school, we know how to get in and out without been seen," Denny said laughing, "We got this Paul, you don't have to worry about us. We will be as quiet as a church mouse."

"Where in Aussie are we going Paul?" Molly and Peter asked together. "Nullarbor, to the Bunda Cliffs, also known as the..." "End of the world," Denny jumps in, "it's on the top of my bucket list of places to visit."

"I'm not sure which chain you will be looking for there but if you work together, you'll figure it when you get there," Paul announced.

As we left the lair, I had a great idea but before I could say anything Alice did, "Guys, what if we drive to the airport and use the cars to turn into an aeroplane and fly to Australia instead using the jetpacks. Three cars will turn into a jet and autopilot will take us there."

I forgot about her powers of mental manipulation which included telepathy. "Alice, is there any way you can stay out our heads?" I laugh.

"Sorry Jackie, I can't help it sometime. I'll try my best to stay out," Alice assured me, "The idea was Jackie's, y'all. Sometimes I forget my powers work on their own and as soon as an idea or something pops into my head, I speak before I check if it was mine or someone else."

"Paul, we are taking three cars and driving to the airport to fly by plane instead," Peter spoke into his watch, "It would be less conspicuous than using our jetpacks." "Be safe," Paul responded.

"Boys you split into two and get to know each other. Us five girls are going together," Molly announced. As we all ran for the vehicles, the boys got to Lamborghinis while the girls vehicles turned into a Jaguar XE S. Three very cool cars.

Molly, Denny, and Rachel jumped into the back of the car. "Guys, you know I can't drive right?" I was so confused.

The girls laughed as Alice looked at me, "I'm driving Jackie, don't worry." They were still laughing at me as Alice, and I got into the car. Peter and Jaden were going together, and Mike and Nick were going together.

Just as the boys were getting into the cars, "Guys, the ISA leaves a few cars in the airport, so you only need to take two," Paul said through the watch.

All the boys jump into a second Jaguar XE S together with Nick driving and Peter in the passenger seat and Mike and Jaden in the back seat.

"Boys first one to the airport, doesn't have to fly the plane," Denny scrammed out the window as Alice drove down the lane as fast as she could.

We race down by the Gaelscoil and turned right into town. Just after the grotto we turned left and down across the new bridge and onto the airport.

It normally takes an hour and half to get to the airport but with how fast Alice was driving, it was going to be so much quicker. Alice was driving way over the speed limit at nearly 200km and the boys were nowhere to be seen behind us.

"So Alice, how long have you been with ISA?" I asked thinking I would pass the time. "Well, Nick and I are both twenty-two and we were both recruited at eight just like these guys were. We were never released from training as early as these guys were.

"We were assigned at eighteen to protect these guys in their school without letting them know. We are both qualified Specials Needs Assistants and the school needed SNA's, so the cover was perfect."

"That's so cool, so you always knew but were not allowed to let them know? Where you surprised when I joined up so late?" I quizzed Alice as we drove to the airport.

"Yes, we always knew but we were there to protect without our identities becoming known. I always knew you were going to become and agent Jackie, I just didn't know when you would become one. Funny story though Peter almost caught myself and Nick talking about the agency in school one day."

Denny, Molly, and Rachel joined in now, "Peter did what?" they all asked shock.

"Yeah, we were in a classroom that was empty for one class, having a chat about how to keep our identity safe because it was getting harder and harder trying to hide it in class.

"My powers come in so handy sometimes. We are only allowed to use our powers on others if we about to be found out. Peter won't remember this, but I modified his memory at that point. He walked in just as Mike said the ISA in the conversation. I normally hear people coming but I was so focused on Nick and the conversation.

"And there Peter stood staring at us with his mouth hanging opened. Nick and I were in complete shock as well. We looked at each other and nodded. And I said, 'I'll do it,' Nick just knew what I had to do.

"Peter looked at me and I told him to forget what he saw and heard for the last few minutes. Peter shook his head and looked at us. 'Sorry, I have class in here next, but I'll wait outside and let the teacher know.' With that sorted we finished the conversation and decided to never talk in school again.

"We did spend the next few days checking on Peter to make sure he never remembered or said anything to anyone. He kept asking us if we were going to be his new SNA's. I knew he was thinking what was happening, he thought there was something wrong with him."

We were all hysterical, we didn't realised we were nearly on the M11 until we were stopped by the Gardaí. There was a check point just before the motorway.

As we got closer to the Gardaí , we rolled down all four windows just in case they wanted to talk to us all.

Irish Spy Agency (ISA) Chronicles Book 2: Chain Retrieval

"Hey ladies, how are you today? Detective O'Malley here," the garda spoke, "Do you have any ID's on you by any chance? You miss, proof of insurance too please."

"Can I reach for the insurance in the glove box?" Alice asked as she handed him her ID. "No need ladies," Detective O'Malley, said as he stared at our ID's, "Didn't realise you were from the Irish Bureau of Investigation."

"Are you related to Detective Bonnie Brown?" the ban garda who had a pin with Garda Smith on it, asked Rachel as she was looking at her ID. "Yes, she is my mother," Rachel answered.

"One of the best detectives, I've ever seen, I hope to be like her one day," Rachel couldn't help but blush as the officer Smith spoke. We all knew Rachel was really proud of her mother.

"You are free to go," both gardaí said, "Hope you can finish your case."

As we drove off and got on the M11, Alice closed her eyes for a few seconds. "Sorry I was just letting the guys know about the check point."

"Alice how does your power of mental manipulation work?" Denny asked. "I have a lot of powers included in the mental manipulation. Reading minds, moving things with my mind including my body, make people not see me or see what I want them to see.

"Especially, when I can see what the biggest fear is and actually make them see it. It's so useful in

Irish Spy Agency (ISA) Chronicles Book 2: Chain Retrieval

battle," she said laughing. We all joined in when all of sudden Alice slammed on the breaks.

"What's wrong Alice?" we all screamed as we grabbed onto the car whatever way we could as Alice lifted up the car and over the barrier we went. She turned the car around to head back to Enniscorthy.

"The guys are in big trouble. The Gardaí stopped them and made them all get out of the car. Something to do with Peter being a wanted man."

Alice went even faster back towards to the guys, swerving in and around cars. She was driving so much fast than the 200km we were going to beat the guys. When I looked at the speedometer it was trying to reach over 300km.

"Alice if you can keep us going straight and going through the other cars, I'll turn us invisible to keep the other cars safe," I questioned. "Let's do it," she answered, "The guys are in big trouble, even though they have shown their badges like we did."

We both did what we needed to do and got back to the guys within five minutes. The Garda had Peter on the ground in cuffs and the others up against the car in cuffs.

"Detective O'Malley, Officer Smith, what's going on?" Molly asked. "Ladies, what are you doing here?" Garda Smith questioned. "The guys are with us. They are working the case with us?" Molly answered.

Irish Spy Agency (ISA) Chronicles Book 2: Chain Retrieval

"They are all free go except Peter," Detective O'Malley responded, "He is a wanted man for the trouble and murders in Enniscorthy the last couple of weeks."

"Ah Detective O'Malley, that was all a misunderstanding," Alice spoke, "Peter was undercover, trying to find the leader of the guys we are trying to get. Unfortunately, I can't go into detail of the case but that much I can tell you."

Both garda nodded at Alice and walked back to their car. "Alice, what's happening?" we all asked confused.

"I've convinced them to let Peter go, they are just letting the Garda commissioner know about the mix up." Within seconds, Detective O'Malley and Garda Smith came back.

"The commissioner has decided to let him go and every Guard has been told to take down the wanted posters," Detective O'Malley announced, " We explained to him what happen and the bit of the case you explained, and he is happy to let you all go. We wish you all the best with the rest of the case."

We help the guards remove the handcuffs from all the men, "Thank you Detective O'Malley and Garda Smith. We do apologise for the mix up."

As we all got back into the cars , we wave at the guards, and we were off. Both cars invisible and speeding off to the airport.

Irish Spy Agency (ISA) Chronicles Book 2: Chain Retrieval

We made it to the airport in like twenty minutes and as we were invisible, we followed signs that only agents of ISA would see.

In and around loads of bends we finally stopped in a car park with loads of different types of vehicles. Limousines, hummers, trucks, and sports cars. And so many more that I had no idea what they were.

Molly jumped out of our car and into another, "I'll meet you on the runway." Off we went to the runway.

The runway surprised me. Because everyone one of them was so full. "Guys how are we going to get our plane on the runway?" I quizzed.

"Jackie, have you not learnt anything yet? With my powers anything is possible," Alice joked, "Now come on, we got to line these cars up in a row. Then they will do the rest."

I knew the cars transformed into whatever vehicle was need at that time, but I didn't think they would turn into a jet.

With Alice driving the first car, Nick in the middle and Molly driving at the back, we were in a line when suddenly, we all together inside a plane.

Nine seats around the edge of the plane with loads of space in the aisle. "So who is flying the plane?" I asked everyone.

"These fine pilots are flying us there and these fine ladies and gentlemen are going to serves us food and drinks while we are flying," Alice spoke as two people entered the plane dressed as pilots and nine flight attendants followed them.

"Jackie, the company have pilots and flight attendants on standby in case we need to leave the country," Molly explained, "We all have a flight attendant to serve each of us."

"Captain Susan and Captain Edmund," The female pilot introduce herself and her co-pilot, "It's nice to finally meet you all, Paul told us you were coming." Before we could answer them though they were already heading to the flight deck.

The flight attendants separated and came to stand by each of us. There was a lot of murmuring going on, so I concentrated on the flight attendant in front of me.

"Is mise Seán, Aon rud atá uait Jackie, cuir glaoch ar m'ainm agus gheobhaidh mé duit é." Oh an Irish speaking flight attendant. This is very cool. "Go raibh míle maith agat Seán. Ar ndóigh déanfaidh mé Seán."

I never get to use my Irish very much, so this is going to be awesome. For those who do not understand Irish, Seán introduces himself to me and told me if I needed anything to call his name. I answered: Thanks a million and of course I would Seán.

All the flight attendants gathered together after this. They did have their own private area on the plane.

Irish Spy Agency (ISA) Chronicles Book 2: Chain Retrieval

"How long is it going to take us to get to Aussie?" I queried. "It would normally take about twenty hours or more to get there but flying with the ISA about thirty minutes. But even less time now because I'm here," Alice answered.

"Jackie turn us invisible," Molly as soon as she said that we all rushed to get the seat belts on as Alice froze in seat staring towards the flight deck.

We flew through the sky at light speed. Alice knew what she was doing, her powers were awesome. The powers we all had were great in their own way, some had more active powers than others but without each other the were useless.

I knew we would arrive at Nullarbor in no time. "Are we there yet?" I inquired. Which sent everyone into a fit of giggles including Alice. Who lost control of the plane while laughing. We did slow down, and it was great thig we did.

As soon as Alice let go of the plane, the pilots had us swerving left and right and turning upside down. Then we could hear what was happening to us.

We were being attacked. Canon's of fire and earth were being hurled at us. We all looked out of the window and saw the enemy outside. The only good thing happening right now was that we had arrived at the cliffs.

"Right guys, we are going to have to jump out here," Peter explained, "Alice can you sense what powers are down there other than fire and earth?"

Irish Spy Agency (ISA) Chronicles Book 2: Chain Retrieval

"Unfortunately, Daniel is down there with the goons. He is enhancing their powers somehow but then again it is Daniel. He is the most powerful agent to ever work for the ISA.

"He is not fighting though, they have him protected as he enhances the others. I'll take Daniel while you all take the rest."

As we all got out jetpacks on except Molly, Mike, and Alice, "Seán, amach leat anois. Gheobhaidh muid abhaile ar bhealach éigin. Cosain sibh féin. Bí curamach. "

I didn't know Seán, but I did want him to be safe as well as the other flight attendants and the pilots. We all took turns jumping out of the plane.

Starting with Peter and Molly, as the work best as a duo. Denny and Rachel jumped together and so did Alice and Nick, Jaden grabbed me and pulled me out and Mike jumped last.

As I flying down, I glanced back up at the plane as it zoomed out of here. We had no idea how we were going to get home, but at least Seán and everyone on the plane were safe.

I noticed there was a load more goons on the ground than were used to, as we landed. We knew we were going to be fighting, landing in a line with Peter in the middle, Molly on the left side of him, followed by Rachel, Mike, and Jaden.

Denny and myself were to the right of Peter, with Alice beside me and Nick on her other side. As

Irish Spy Agency (ISA) Chronicles Book 2: Chain Retrieval

we got ready to fight, we all noticed Daniel on the other side. He was surrounded by goons.

"While Alice is getting Daniel, the rest of us will attack the rest and keep them off Alice," Peter commanded, "Let's go."

As we ran forward, the goons ran for us. Flipping over each other, kicking ass, using our powers to keep the goons off Alice, who disappeared. Looking towards Daniel, he was concentrating on something.

"Alice, I know you can hear me. What is Daniel up to? He is too focus on something and not fighting." I spoke in my head. Something is wrong, I can feel it.

"Guys, we need to get them out of here. Daniel has them keeping us busy so he can get the chain," I screamed at everyone, "Alice, new plan. Leave Daniel alone and come get these guys off us."

Alice was standing next to me in no time. "Alice I need you to make the goons and Daniel see their worst fears. She nodded and went to work. As I stared at her, she floating up in the air.

As she was flying above us all, she placed her hands in front of her. Every one of the goons, screamed in agony.

"Get them off." "Let me out of here." "Help me, I'm drowning." Focusing on Daniel, he was screaming something else. "It's all my fault. Their dead because of me. It's my fault." He was bawling and slapping his hands on his head at this point.

Irish Spy Agency (ISA) Chronicles Book 2: Chain Retrieval

As they were screaming most of them starting to retreat out of there, grabbing Daniel as they walked by him. Within twenty seconds they had all gone.

We formed a circle to keep watch for a few minutes to make sure they would not be back.

"There is no chain here guys. Something else is here altogether. I'm not sure yet but it's definitely something to do with the ISA," I spoke up, "Daniel was the only one looking and with his memory gone, he wouldn't be looking for a chain."

"Jackie's right lads," Peter announced, "Daniel would have known Paul was searching for the chains but when his memories disappeared, he would have forgotten."

"Something is telling me that Denny, Jaden, Mike, and Rachel, your powers are the only ones needed here," I said, "The rest of us will surround you and protect you."

Denny, Jaden, Mike, and Rachel stood together and took a step out from each other, like a compass they were standing north, south, east, and west. The rest of us circle them about ten feet away.

"How do we do this?" Mike questioned. "Focus on each other and on each other's powers," I shouted at them.

Closing their eyes, they reached their hands in the air pointing at each other. Nothing was

Irish Spy Agency (ISA) Chronicles Book 2: Chain Retrieval

happening. Idiot! I'm such an idiot. "Jackie, you're not an idiot. Look!" Alice told me.

Looking at Denny, Mike, Jaden, and Rachel, there was a light coming from each of them and connected in the middle. The light went up to the sky and then back down.

Chuckling to myself, it was like a rainbow. As I saw it land though I noticed something.

"Guys, that's where Daniel was standing," I screamed as we all raced over to the end of the light.

The ground had opened up slowly but what was there was not what we were expecting at all. It wasn't the chain but a piece of paper with the ISA logo on it.

So it did belong to us, but we had no idea what it was. "Let's bring it back to Paul, he might know what it is," Peter spoke quietly.

"How are we going to do that Peter?" Rachel questioned, "Our plane has already left." Alice and Nick started laughing now.

In between laughing Mike spoke, "Our company watches have a feature. We can open portals to go anywhere in the world. Did Paul never tell you this?" "He never said a thing," Mike answered.

"Well, it's possible Paul never knew about it," Alice announced, "We were also never told but my power help us find out. It only works in emergency situations like this."

Irish Spy Agency (ISA) Chronicles Book 2: Chain Retrieval

Alice and Nick both pressed the buttons on their watches and pointed in front of us. They closed their eyes and a weird looking vortex thing open in front of us.

I walked towards the side of it to look behind it, but nothing was there. "Well , if I remember anything from movies and books about vortexes or portals is that we have to have a clear picture of we want to go or we could end up anywhere," I stated.

"And I do mean anywhere, space, the ocean , a volcano. Picture Paul's lair or even Vinegar hill extremely clear and we won't die. It's that simple. Are you all ready?"

With eight heads nods, we slowly walked into the vortex portal. An image of Paul's lair popped into my head. Knowing it was Alice, an idea came to me. Alice and I glanced at each other and smirked. She knew my plan, but I knew she wasn't going to say anything. This was going to be a hilarious.

Chapter 2: The Map

    Entering Paul's lair on the other end of the vortex portal, I could see everyone, but they couldn't see me.
    I turned myself invisible to have a bit of fun with the agents. With Alice in on it, this is going to be amazing. We do need a bit of fun in our lives at the moment.
    The moment was coming. I noticed everyone was looking around the lair to make sure we all got back.
    "Jackie," Molly screamed, "Guys, where's Jackie? She didn't come through." They all started screaming my name. but I thought I would play on it for another few minutes.

Irish Spy Agency (ISA) Chronicles Book 2: Chain Retrieval

"I'm going to check up above," Denny said as she ran out the door. "Wait until she comes back Jackie," Alice told me in my head.

They were all get frantic now. "Jackie, could be anywhere." "Jackie's dead, she went to space and exploded." These were only the two things I heard because they were screaming something.

Denny came back at this point, "She is not up there. Are we 100% sure she came through the vortex portal with us, or did she end up going somewhere else?"

"We can't have lost Jackie too," Rachel screamed on the verge of tears. As I was about to turn back visible, Alice screamed at me in my head, "Now, Jackie."

"Boo," I screamed as I turned visible. Alice, Paul, and I started laughing while the others were not so happy with me. They actually looked angry with me.

"Guys, come on I was joking," I said in between laughter, "We needed some fun in our lives at the moment."

Still getting daggers off the guys, I started to feel horrible. "Never mind them Jackie," Alice and Paul spoke up, "They never know when to have fun in life."

Still feeling bad but as I look at Paul and Alice they had an evil grin on their faces. "What are you two up too?" I questioned them.

Irish Spy Agency (ISA) Chronicles Book 2: Chain Retrieval

They never answered but smiled bigger. "Why is getting so cold in here?" I quizzed. Alice and Paul were busy daydreaming to answer me.

The room got colder and colder and I was absolutely shivering. Notice the other two were shivering. Then something hit me.

As the shock wore off, I did notice the floor was gone and it was covered in snow. Now the fun begins.

Picking up some snow and making a ball, "Snowball fight," I screamed as I threw my ball at Molly. As snowballs were flying back and forth, laughter filled the air. Everyone was having so much fun, including Paul.

Forgetting about everything that has happen in last few days and months. This feeling growing inside me was amazement.

This went on for about twenty minutes. Snowman and snow angels. It was a snow day but inside, crazy but awesome.

As we were all worn out and lying in the snow, it slowly started to disappear. Alice and Paul were daydreaming once again as the rest of us caught our breath.

"What chain did you all find?" Paul inquired. "The funny thing Paul," Denny began, "There was no chain."

"What do you mean?" Paul questioned. "Well, Daniel was there with loads of the goons," I began, "They attacked the plane we were on, so we sent the pilots and flight attendants away and we went to fight."

"Daniel was being protected so we made a plan of attack. Alice made them all see their worst fears. Which was hilarious in my opinion," Jaden announced.

"Including Daniel, which was needed because he was focus on finding something," Mike spoke, "As they all left Jackie gave us the new plan."

"She had a feeling, that Jaden, Mike, Rachel, and myself were the key to getting the chain," Denny continued, "The four of stood like a compass and focused on each other and our powers."

"It worked," Peter spoke, "A light came from each of them and went straight into the sky."

"It was like a rainbow," Molly said, "The light came down and landed exactly where Daniel was standing."

"The ground slowly disappeared," Alice stated, "And in its place was this piece of paper." Nick handed Paul the paper. "We don't know what it means. Do you?"

As Paul stared at the paper with the ISA logo on it. "I have no idea, but we figure it out. And we'll figure it out fast as we are together," Paul spoke, "The ISA loves teamwork."

We spent the whole afternoon studying the paper and researching on the internet as well as looking through old ISA files that Paul has in his office.

Irish Spy Agency (ISA) Chronicles Book 2: Chain Retrieval

Looking through all these newspaper was absolute torture. I have no idea how anyone would research this way. It's horrible, having to read every article trying to find out what the paper was.

This research was killing me, "Anyone hungry?" I asked, "I can run for some food." "Yes," Everyone screamed. "I'll head home and get some. It seems like we will be here for a long time, so I'm thinking a proper dinner. Any request?"

"Pizza." "Lasagne and chips." "Curry and Rice." They were the only three I heard but there was more. "Guys let's stick to one meal," I commanded, "My father is not superman, he can't cook everything by the time I go home.

We all laughed but they all knew I was being serious. "How about lasagne and chips? It's not too light for snack so it will be a meal," I asked.

"Lasagne would be great," Paul spoke up now, he was too quiet while we were researching. "Agreed," everyone shouted.

"Nick and I will go with you," Alice said as I was just ringing my dad, "We want to officially meet your parents and we will drive there instead of flying." I nodded as my dad picked up.

"Hey dad, I was wondering if you could make extra lasagne and chips tonight," I asked, "I'll come and collect." *"How many extra am I cooking for?"*

"Ten," I answered, "And two of them are coming with me. They want to meet you officially."

Irish Spy Agency (ISA) Chronicles Book 2: Chain Retrieval

"See you soon then," My father said as he hung up. Placing my phone in pocket, "We'll back soon guys. You keep researching and we'll be about an hour before the food is ready."

Walking out the door with Alice and Mike on my heels. "Why did you ask what everyone wanted Jackie?" Alice asked, "You already knew what was for dinner." We laughed as we went outside.

I turned all three of us invisible in case people were on Vinegar Hill. Thankfully, there was not. We had to run to the car because it was lashing rain.

As I was opening the back, Nick had opened Alice's door and the passenger door for me, "In here you go," he said. I was always told to let the oldest in the front of the car regardless of gender.

Alice drove to my house which way over at the other side of the town. There was still loads of people walking through the town in the rain.

Crossing one of the two bridges to get over to my house. In Enniscorthy to cross the two bridges it was one big loop. It was a one way system.

Up one hill, driving through the main part of town up another hill. Yes I know. There are way too many hills in Enniscorthy.

The people of Enniscorthy complained about the hills all the time but we never did anything about it. Ironic isn't it. As we were driving though I did notice all the damaged buildings and the ones falling apart.

Irish Spy Agency (ISA) Chronicles Book 2: Chain Retrieval

I had forgotten all about the buildings in town being destroyed when Peter and goons burned them down or whatever they did to them.

They were still loads of people helping to put things back together. The Gardaí were helping, I could the gangs parents all helping. Peter's parents, Isaac and Rosalin, Molly and Denny's parent, Landon and Frankie, Geoffrey Mike's dad and Rachel's mom Bonnie.

Even Daniel's mam Anne with my mother Jessica was there helping. Jaden's dad Stephen and Mike mother Lexi were showing people what to do.

I could see that Stephen and Lexi were running the show which was totally understandable. They were in a construction business together.

My father must at home cooking up a storm for everyone. "We must help your dad over the next hour," Alice announced, "This is one of the reasons why we came with."

"But just between me and you, I can't cook anything," Alice whispered, "We can have tea and let the men cook. Nick is an incredible cook."

This town was absolutely destroyed, thanks to Peter and the goons. But I'm so happy to see the people of Enniscorthy coming together to help rebuild the town.

Now we just have to make sure that the goons won't attack the town with Daniel because there will be no stopping them then. We will just have to think positively about it. But I do have a feeling that

Irish Spy Agency (ISA) Chronicles Book 2: Chain Retrieval

Daniel and the goons are going after the chains as well.

As we pulled into my driveway, I realised I never told Alice where I lived but with her power I didn't need to.

"Hey dad," I called out as I opened my door and walked in. Dad was sweaty when I saw him in the kitchen, "Dad, is everything ok?" I questioned.

"Oh hey sweetheart," Dad answered, "Cooking for hundreds of people in a small kitchen is extremely hard but my restaurant is one of the first buildings being restored.

"As far as I know, it's nearly ready for me to move back into. Much easier to cook for everyone in the kitchen there."

"Dad, this Alice and Nick," I introduced them, "They also work for ISA. Nick is going to help you cook. And he will run the food to the people of the town until you can move back to the restaurant."

Dad shook both of their hands before jumping back into work. Nick had already duplicated himself and jumped in to help. "Dad, take a step back, tell Nick what to do," I told him, "Run the kitchen like the restaurant, Nick won't mind.

Alice and I sat in the kitchen, looking amazed at the two men work as we sipped on our tea. It was incredible.

"Alice, I've been doing a lot of thinking on this piece of paper that we found," I spoke up, "You already know this, but I think it will be Denny,

Irish Spy Agency (ISA) Chronicles Book 2: Chain Retrieval

Jaden, Mike, and Rachel powers' are going to tell us what it is."

"I think we will be looking to you for all our plans in the future," Alice giggled, "You seem to know a lot more than we thought you did. And your plans are the only ones working lately.

"But I agree, their powers' found the paper, so we got to get that light back on it to see what it is."

"I knew you would understand," We both laughed, "We'll get this food back to the gang and then we will get them to use their powers on the paper."

We continued to chat about nonsense for a few minutes before Nick handed us a bag. "This is for the gang," he said, "I'm going to stay behind and help your dad. I'll help even more when we move to the restaurant.

"I can help there more until you guys need me and then I can still stay behind and help but you will get the real me." He laughed as he was walking out the door with another bag.

"We'll take those to everyone as we drive buy," no need for us all to go the same way if you're going to stay," I said taking the bags off Nick.

"Thanks, Heath," Alice said, "It was nice to meet you. Enjoy getting to know Nick." I kissed my father on the cheek and said see you later as Alice kissed Nick goodbye.

Irish Spy Agency (ISA) Chronicles Book 2: Chain Retrieval

Alice drove us through the town and over to my mother and Anne. "Hey mom," I shouted, and she looked at me as Alice and I unloaded the boot.

My mother and Anne came over to help, they told us to follow them as they brought the lunch over to the canopy where the food was to be served.

"Have you guys come to help?" Anne questioned.

"Unfortunately not," Alice answered, "We have go to get back to the others, but my husband Nick will be by soon with more food, He stayed behind to help Heath cook but he has the power of duplication."

I hugged my mother goodbye as Alice, and I got back into the car. We drove as fast as we could back up to Vinegar Hill so the food would not go cold.

But it didn't work, the food was cold. We both ran up the hill towards the castle. Alice had lifted me up onto the top and as she landed beside we both back flipped off in Paul's lair.

"This has been the most fun, I have ever had," I said as we walk into the main room with the gang. Alice just laughed but I knew she knew what I meant.

"What took you so long?" Denny quizzed us, "We have being going mad here with hunger." Everyone laughed.

Irish Spy Agency (ISA) Chronicles Book 2: Chain Retrieval

"Sorry," I began, "We brought food for everyone who is helping re-build this town. Nick decided to stay and help my dad cook but he will be back here soon."

"Denny we are going to need your help," Alice started to explain but was interrupted by Denny, "The food got cold?" We both nodded.

As Denny too the bag off us Alice spoke to Paul, "Paul, I think Jackie is looking for a promotion," we both laughed as the rest were confused, "She has come up with a plan to see what is on that paper. And as soon as we eat she will tell you all."

Denny had fire covering her hand as she walked by the table she placed the food on, placing her hand over each tray of lasagne and chips.

"Dig in everyone," I spoke, "Dad made the lasagne from scratch." We all sat at the table and chairs that Paul had brought out for us.

"What's this plan you came up?" Denny questioned while we were eating. I knew someone was going to ask.

"Well, Alice is going to make the paper float," I explained, "Then Denny, Jaden, Mike, and Rachel, you are going to use your powers at the same time and direct them on to the paper. Just like in Aussie when you came together to find the paper."

"Sounds great Jackie," Peter spoke up, "I might let you make all the plans from now on." We all laughed. I was unsure if Peter was being sincere or not.

Irish Spy Agency (ISA) Chronicles Book 2: Chain Retrieval

We finished eating and everything was cleared away before we can take a breath. I forgot Paul had super speed. Everyone got into to place fast. I think we were all eager to find out what this piece of paper was.

Alice was pointing at the paper, and it was floating in the middle of Denny, Jaden, Mike, and Rachel.

Mike pointed two fingers at towards the paper and a tornado came out of them and hit the paper. Denny made a fist and hit the paper with fire. Jaden made a claw and sent some brick, mud, stone, and other things at the paper.

Rachel hands was kind of weird, but sent a waterfall of sorts at the paper. Her index and middle finger made a 'v' pointing up, another 'v' at the side and her thumbs was the side.

Within seconds something started to appear on the piece of paper.

'Irish Spy Agency Retrieval Map.'

They stopped using their powers as Paul grabbed the map and flipped it over. "There is no map though," Paul spoke, "*'Irish Spy Agency Retrieval Map of Lost Chains,'* is the only thing on it."

Peter grabbed it off Paul in frustration and the map changed. In place of the words was a picture of Hookhead Lighthouse in Churchtown Co

Irish Spy Agency (ISA) Chronicles Book 2: Chain Retrieval

Wexford. A forty minute drive away from Enniscorthy.

"Paul, Hookhead is on here," Peter stated. Paul took a look at the map and saw Hookhead too but as soon as he touched it, it was back to the words.

"I think it depends on our powers," I began to explain as I took the map of Paul, "The map will change with whoever is holding it. Peter's chain is at Hookhead while mine is at the Sistine Chapel in the painting on the ceiling.

"Each of us will hold the map," I continued, "And let us know exactly where we are going."

I handed the map to Denny because she was standing beside. "Underwater volcanos at Mariana Trench." Denny passed it to Alice.

"Jacob's Ladder in Texas to the moon," Alice announced a bit confused as she passed it to Molly who looked even more. "It just says the atmosphere."

"Molly that would be a piece of land in the sky somewhere that the ISA lost thousands of years. We will research it while you are finding the rest," Paul assured her.

Molly handed the map to Rachel, "Mariana Trench." She high five Denny who was extremely happy that she was not going to be alone. Rachel handed the map to Jaden, " The Great Pyramid of Giza."

Irish Spy Agency (ISA) Chronicles Book 2: Chain Retrieval

Mike took the map out of Jaden's Hands and said, "Alice, I'm coming with you, Jacob's Ladder in the Texas to the moon."

We never noticed Nick walking in until he asked Mike for the map. "Hippodrome Aeon Circus, Galway Hall of Mirrors."

"Awesome," I declared, "We all know where we are going to and we will find out where Molly has to go. Now we just have to decide where we are going first."

"What do you mean, Jackie?" Denny questioned, "We will be so much quicker if we go ourselves to pick up our own chains."

"That makes the most sense Denny," I answered, "That's what Daniel and the goons will want. They'll be expecting us on our so it will be easier to take the chains off us when we get them. We are stronger together."

"Jackie's right," Paul said, "Travel together it might take longer but it is safer. Especially now that the world knows who you are as well. Safer for you all as well as the public."

"We'll head towards Mariana Trench," Peter announced, "It's the most dangerous. We will help Denny and Rachel get their chains and get out. Then we will go from there."

"Let's head back to the airport get the jet to fly over the Mariana trench," Molly said, "Alice can make it look like the jet is not there and we all fly

Irish Spy Agency (ISA) Chronicles Book 2: Chain Retrieval

down with the jet packs and help Denny and Rachel."

As we ran out the screaming a goodbye to Paul, might be a few days before we see him again. Alice and Nick drove again as we all piled in. Ladies in one car and the men in the other.

There was no stopping us this time, I turned both cars invisible and Alice and Nick drove about two hundred kilometres over the speed limit. But we did not care about that.

This mission was the number one priority for us because it was going to help us get Daniel back too.

We made it to the airport in even less time than before. As the jet formed the same crew as before walk on.

"Séan, conas atá tú? Táim an-sásta gur éirigh leat go léir ar ais slán," I said hugging him. I asked him how he was, and I told him I was so glad he got back safe.

"Tá mé go maith Jackie," (I'm good, Jackie.) he answered, "Bhí a fhois agam go mbeadh an post seo rud beag contúirteach ach is breá liom é." (I knew this job was dangerous, but I love it.

"Bíodh suíochán agat agus inis dom fút féin." (Sit down and tell me about yourself.) As a seat appeared beside me, Séan sat down.

We had a lovely conversation as Gaeilge about his family and his love for travel and how plans on bringing his wife, Saoirse and kids, Jack, Mark,

Irish Spy Agency (ISA) Chronicles Book 2: Chain Retrieval

Clodagh, and Clare on a trip around the world when he has saved enough to buy a jet.

'We have arrived.' The captain spoke over the speaker. I could see the look on Séan's and the other flight attendants. "Ná bí buartha. (Don't worry.) Beidh sibh go léir sábháiltean uair seo. (You are safe this time.) Geallaim duit Séan. (I promise you, Séan." I reassured him.

As we all got our jetpacks on, "You all need to sit down and strap up." Alice told the flight attendants but Séan had no idea what she said, "Séan, ní mór duit go léir suí síos agus strap suas." I translated and Séan nodded and sat down.

As they all strapped in Alice opened the door. The wind was pulling us towards the door so fast, "Mike," we all screamed.

Mike slowed down the wind enough for us to walk to the door and jump out. We jumped out one by one. Alice, Peter, Nick, Molly, Denny, Rachel, Jaden, myself, and Mike last.

As soon as Mike jumped out, Alice closed the door to keep the flight attendants and pilots safe. She always made the plane disappear. I turned invisible to see if I could I see it, but it was like it wasn't there.

Chapter 3: Mariana Trench

From above the Mariana trench looked incredible. A big, huge circle under the water with an enormous drop.

"Jackie, Jaden, and Mike you are going under with Denny and Rachel," Peter commanded, "The rest of us will stay up here and not let anyone down."

As the five of us dived into the ocean, Mike had oxygen bubble covering our heads. "We can chat and keep an eye on each other now," He said to us as dived deeper.

"Denny and Rachel, you need to focus on your powers, and it will lead you to the chain," I announced, "Where to first?"

Irish Spy Agency (ISA) Chronicles Book 2: Chain Retrieval

"Rachel, you go first," Denny said, "We are in your element, so your chain could be the furthest away. I see the underwater volcano, so I feel like that's where I'm going."

Rachel closed her eyes to focus. It took a few minutes, but she started to move deeper into the depths.

"My element is drawing me to the chain," Rachel said, "Follow me." We all swam after her.

The further down we went the darker it got. I'm not the best swimmer. I pressed the buttons on my watch, "Torch."

The strongest light I have ever seen appeared. I turned 360° to see where everyone was. I was alone, the others had disappeared.

I knew not to panic because I wanted to survive. All the goblin sharks swimming around me though were cool. I absolutely love sharks.

They were some ugly fish swimming around too. Vampire squid, Telescope Octopi, Viperfish, Anglerfish, and some Black Dragonfish. These fish were more terrifying than the sharks.

"Jackie, down here," Mike called. As looked down, one of the goblin sharks swam by me. I've never been so close to a shark before. It was incredible.

I swam down towards the others. Having to stop a couple of times before I reached the others as the fish and sharks swam by me an inch away.

Irish Spy Agency (ISA) Chronicles Book 2: Chain Retrieval

"Rachel is still going," Mike said as I caught up, "We are nearly at the bottom of trench now at thirty-six thousand, two hundred and one feet deep. That's at an eleven thousand and thirty-four metres deep." Mike tagged the last bit on because I looked extremely confused.

I normally only swim at the swimming pool. This is definitely all new to me, but I really enjoyed being outside my comfort zone.

With the light we could see everything better. Rachel had come to a stop. "It's around here somewhere," Rachel shouted, "I can feel it."

Rachel's entire bodied disappeared for a second. She became one with the water. Amazing. When she re-appeared she was wearing the chain.

The chain was unbelievable breathtaking. It was just a normally silver chain with a wave pendant on it. The difference between this chain though is the waves move.

"You did it Rachel," Denny screamed, "The chain looks incredible on you."

"Your turn now Denny," I said, "We know where your chain is but focus on your power and it will draw you in."

Denny did the same as Rachel, she closed her eyes and was pulled towards the underwater volcano. We followed her.

This time I didn't get lost, we had my torch still showing the way. We did a lot of swimming around the sharks and the fish this time. There was a lot more of them around.

"Guys, what is happening up there?" I screamed into the watch, "We are being surrounded by sharks and fish."

"*Daniel and the goons are here,*" Alice shouted back, "*Daniel has the sharks and fish going after you.*"

"Rachel's got her chain," Mike spoke, "We'll send her up and we'll stay with Denny she nearly has her chain too."

Rachel propelled herself out of the water, it was cool to see. The chain has already starting working for her. The sharks and fish followed her up to.

"These chains are awesome," I said as we continued to follow Denny. Who had also disappeared at this point.

Mike, Jaden, and I stayed outside the underwater volcano, we just knew that's where Denny went to get her chain.

Just like Rachel, Denny came out of the volcano with her chain around her neck with a fire pendant on it and the flames were moving.

"Let's get up there," Jaden shouted, "The team needs us." The watches picked up that one and propelled us straight up towards the team.

As we came out of the water, the fight was happening but only Rachel was fighting this time. Alice, Nick, Peter, and Molly were floating in the air watching. They did look gobsmacked.

Irish Spy Agency (ISA) Chronicles Book 2: Chain Retrieval

Rachel's control over water had intensified so much she was just floating the air with her eyes closed. It was like her power changed to telekinesis.

The pacific ocean had raised over 200 feet in the air. Rachel had created a tsunami, but she only hit Daniel and the goons with it.

"My turn," Denny said smirking as she flew up beside Rachel. She closed her eyes too. These chains had enormous power and I'm glad we found them instead of Daniel and the goons.

The fun had just begun for Denny as her powers had created fireballs the size of meteorites. She threw them at the goons.

The ocean underneath started to shake, and it opened up. When we looked down it had opened over the volcano that Denny went into.

"Get back," I screamed. Knowing this wasn't Rachel. Denny was just about to make the volcano erupt. We all moved back out of the way just in time.

The volcano erupted and just as it went up past us, it hit something in the air and changed direction and headed towards Daniel and the goons.

Daniel deflected it but it hit some of the goons. This fight was indescribable. It was going from bad to worse for the goons.

They also reached for each other hands and that's when everything changed for the goons and Daniel.

Irish Spy Agency (ISA) Chronicles Book 2: Chain Retrieval

Denny and Rachel both opened their eyes, it was definitely different. The iris and the white part of Denny and Rachel's eyes were gone.
Denny's eyes were completely red, and Rachel's had become navy blue. It matched their agency uniforms.
The weather changed, dark clouds, thunder and lightning, which struck all the goons. They were all vapourised. Daniel was gone too. But I don't think he was hit, he must have transported out.
Denny and Rachel had come back to us excited. "This is awesome," Denny said, "Where are we off to next?"
"It is safer to head back to Paul and explain everything to him," I suggested, "We can't keep searching for the chains while Daniel and the goons keep showing up and attacking."
The all pondered what I said, and all agreed. Alice made the plane re-appear as we flew up towards it.
Alice had the already opened the door before we got to it. In we went one by one util we were all sitting down.
The seats were different this time around though. The seats were round a table. "Time for food," one of the flight attendants said.
A vermicelli pasta dish appeared in front of us. It looked and smelled delicious. "Taitneamh a bhaint as gach duine," Séan said. The pilots flew us home as we ate.

Irish Spy Agency (ISA) Chronicles Book 2: Chain Retrieval

"Séan, an féidir leat iarraidh ar an bpíolóta sinn a eitilt thar chiseal Phóil, le do thoil?" I asked Séan to ask the pilots to drop us over Paul's lair.

Séan went straight to the pilots. "Guys, I have asked Séan to ask the pilots to drop us over Paul's lair instead of flying to the airport," I announced.

"Hey Jackie," Molly spoke up while everyone was giggling, "We all speak fluent Gaeilge. We can speak every language fluently including every countries sign language."

Everyone was laughing at me, so I joined in. I knew they meant well.

"Tá na píolótaí chun tú a scaoileadh amach thar ciseal Phóil, (The pilots are going to drop you all off over Paul's lair.)" Séan said as he came back.

The food tasted amazing, but we were back over Paul's lair in no time.

"Last to land in the lair has to wash the outside of all our houses," Denny screamed as she jumped out first. It was race but I knew I wanted to be the first one there. I hate washing the outside of my own house.

I was unfortunately the last out of the plane, but I knew what I had to do. I created a border in the air that surrounded the others and flew them back up towards the plane as it flew away.

The agents had no way out not even Alice. I laughed as I landed in the castle and down in Paul's lair.

Irish Spy Agency (ISA) Chronicles Book 2: Chain Retrieval

"What has you laughing?" Paul questioned me. "Denny wanted a race down from the plane and the loser had power-wash all our houses," I answered, "I didn't want to lose so I stopped them using an invisible border that brought them up instead of down."

"Ah I see," Paul replied, "You're taking to using your powers extremely fast. Quicker than the rest did when they started off."

"Daniel helped a little with the training," I said, "And plus I wanted to learn quick so I could help the team."

"You are such a cheater," Denny screamed at me while walking into the lair. Paul and I were too busy laughing at them to answer.

Denny, Alice, Nick, Peter, Molly, Jaden, Mike, and Rachel was last to arrive in the lair. Lucky for her she controls water. She can wash all the houses at once.

"What are you guy doing back here?" Paul asked as Rachel walked in.

"Jackie, thought it would be best to come back after we got the two chains," Molly announced, "Especially since Daniel and the goons are always turning up."

"That's the best plan and we can decide where to go next soon," Paul spoke, "With Daniel we could always lead them a stray.

"Until then Molly," Paul continued, "The piece of land that you have to go to is called Carabalk Isle. It was a piece of land that was discovered by the ISA, when the ISA was formed six thousand years ago."

"I remember studied about pieces of land that the ISA lost at Camp Duo when we were studying," Rachel announced, "Carabalk Isle was discovered by Diana, the wife of Dean, the founder of the ISA.

"She discovered an island floating in the sky while she was on plane. She sent the location to her husband but by the time he flew up there it was gone.

"They spent years trying to find it. Dean was hundred and sixty when they re-discovered it. Once Carabalk Isle is discovered it moves position so no one can find it again, so it was considered lost by ISA in six hundred B.C.

"Dean must have place the flight chain there to stop people like Daniel from being too powerful and unable to stop."

"That's right Rachel," Paul confirmed, "If Daniel or anyone like Daniel got a hold of theses chains, they would be invincible not even I could stop them if they turned bad.

"For now while I do some more research on Carabalk Isle, you guys can head home. Rachel has houses to wash." We all laughed as we headed the door.

"I better get back to Dad," I said as we were flying home, "Make sure he has eaten after coking all day."

Irish Spy Agency (ISA) Chronicles Book 2: Chain Retrieval

I was in a daze the whole home. These last few weeks has been crazy. From joining the Irish Spy Agency to Peter getting kidnapped, to us bringing him back and Daniel getting kidnapped.

I think I need to crash but I'm too worried and too worked up to sleep properly. I'll sleep when we get Daniel back.

Rachel had already started power washing our houses before we landed. Theses chains are incredible. One big wave washed all the houses at once. Front and back of the houses were done.

I ran inside to find my father, but he wasn't in the house. Taking out my phone to ring either my mother or father. I decided to ring my mother because if dad wasn't here, the restaurant must be officially done.

"Hey Mam," I spoke as she answered the phone, "How is everything going? Do you all need any help?"

"Hey honey, it's all going good. Dad is in the restaurant cooking up a storm for dinner again with Nick. We can use all the help you can offer. Quick question how can Nick be in two places at once?"

"Nick can be in as many places as he wants," I laughed as I explained, "The power Nick got when he joined the ISA was duplication."

"Ah that's so cool," She said, "You should ask how that works. I mean when you get your powers and how your power choose you."

Irish Spy Agency (ISA) Chronicles Book 2: Chain Retrieval

"I'll bring the gang around as soon as Rachel washes our houses," I could hear laughing on the other end of the line, "I'll explain when we get there."

I got wet as soon as I walked outside. Rachel had a wave of water hitting all our houses at once. They all fell over laughing at me.

It was like I was standing under a waterfall as Alice wouldn't let me move either. They got their payback from me cheating jumping out of the plane.

I never saw anyone else on the estate leave their house ever. So I always wondered who live there. They all must work for the ISA because no one is running out of their houses wondering what is happening.

Maybe I was destined to join the ISA but because I always felt invisible, to everyone but my parents but it was late happening.

I ran upstairs to change when Rachel finished washes the houses and me. As I pulled clothes out of the wardrobe to change my phone rang.

Pulling clothes off my bed trying to find my phone, I did fall onto the bed. I heard laughing behind me. Alice!

Alice pushed me onto the bed with her mind, so I pulled her towards the bed as well. As we giggled on the bed, my rang again. "Where is that damn phone?" I screeched as I searched. The ring got louder and louder.

Irish Spy Agency (ISA) Chronicles Book 2: Chain Retrieval

Alice was still giggling beside so I looked at her and she was staring at the ceiling. She had my phone floating between us and the ceiling. Reaching for the phone but it moved.
And again, and again.
"Alice if you don't give me my phone, I'll be in big trouble." She giggle as she moved the phone again and again. My parents are the only ones who ring me so I would be in big trouble if I don't answer.
She lowered the phone towards but as soon as I reached for it she pulled it back. "Alice, you are such a child," I giggled. Alice giggled alongside me but gave me the phone.
Dad tried to ring me. Oh crap, I better ring him back.
It went straight to voicemail. "Dad, it's me, Ring me back. Alice was trying to be funny and kept the phone away from me."
"Alice, let's go," I got up and grabbed her by the hand, "We got stuff to do."
"Where we going?" "To help rebuild the town." We ran down the stairs and out to the others. Outside the others were muttering together.
"Let's go guys," I said, "My mother is waiting on us. While we are coming up with a plan, we are going to help re-build this town with everyone else."
Everone nodded. Pressing the button on our watches and said, "Rollerblades." We instantly had

Irish Spy Agency (ISA) Chronicles Book 2: Chain Retrieval

rollerblades on. Each the same colour as our ISA uniforms.

"Last one down the town," I screamed as I skated off. Rachel must have noticed I was a little lost, so she shouted, "Has to wash all the company cars this time."

We were all off.

I was winning, then Alice was winning, Peter, Mike, Molly, Denny, Jaden, and Rachel. Nick didn't really care if he won or lost. At least we know that Alice is as competitive as the rest of us.

It was all changing so fast as we were flying downtown but in the end Alice won and Nick lost. After Alice it was Denny, Jaden, myself, Molly and Rachel joint and Mike.

"Well Nick, you can go wash all the cars whenever you want to," I said as we all laughed. "It's already happening, Jackie," Nick laughed, "I'm already washing them all." We all laughed as we rolled up to my mother.

As the skates disappeared, we all jumped straight into helping. There was a lot of smiles from the people of Enniscorthy as we all slid in to help wherever we could.

Our secret was out so we didn't bother hiding our powers from everyone. Alice was floating in the air moving things in place with her mind and was holding things together as others used drills and screws to keep them together.

Irish Spy Agency (ISA) Chronicles Book 2: Chain Retrieval

Nick was everywhere at once. Denny was melding wood and metal pillars together while Rachel was cooling them down.

Jaden was helping with levelling off the earth and making holes in the ground. Peter was helping carrying things while Molly was helping my mother with the drinks with me.

Mike was kept the air cool because it was so warm. The sun was splitting the trees which is actually very rare for Ireland.

People were happy for the help even from Peter. After all he caused the town to fall apart when he was under the fluence of the goons.

With all the work we were doing, the time flew by. As we worked, I noticed RTÉ news vans pull up out of the corner of my eye.

"Alice, you see what I'm seeing?" I asked in my head. "Yes, I do," Alice responded, "It's alright though. We can answer some of their questions without revealing anything important."

"Let's do it," I said, "I'll follow your leads." We headed to the news crew. We went to them to protect the citizens of Enniscorthy out of harm's way.

I put a shield to protect the people regardless of what was going to happen here. I knew some of these news interviews can get extremely violent.

"Alice, you and Molly do all the talking," I announced, "They'll try to talk to Peter but best to stay out of it. They will rile you up for you to

Irish Spy Agency (ISA) Chronicles Book 2: Chain Retrieval

attack." Every nodded as we continued to walk towards RTÉ news.

"Hello there, I'm Sarah Kelly and this RTÉ news," the woman introduced herself, "Todays guests are the people who partly destroyed the town Enniscorthy, but they also saved the town and now are willing to stay and help re-build the town.

"How are guys able to the things you do? Like fly, control the elements?" "Those we can't answer I'm afraid. But what I can tell you is that we have powers, but we can only use them to protect others.

"The company we work for has to be kept secret to protect them as well as their families." Molly spoke up and Alice continued.

"Yes, there are people out there that don't work for the company anymore and it's our job to stop them while protecting the world. Things have happened while fighting the goons, but I know at end of it all, we will stop it all."

"So, Peter can you tell us what happened when you were kidnapped that one time?" Sarah questioned.

Even though Peter was in charged he was staring at me. I nodded. "To be honest with you Sarah, I'm not sure what happened when I was kidnapped other than I was brainwashed. At the time I thought I was doing right until these guys saved me."

Irish Spy Agency (ISA) Chronicles Book 2: Chain Retrieval

"How did they save you?" Sarah quizzed. "Unfortunately, Sarah that is not relevant here. All you need to know is we lost someone while trying to save Peter, but we are getting him back soon."

"Who is the mystery person that you lost?" Sarah was showing to much interest in us now. We needed to stop this now before anyone got hurt.

"Sarah for the safety of everyone involved, we cannot let you know anymore. It is for your safety just as much." I said, "This interview is over now. Goodbye."

As we walked away Sarah and her camera man followed us.

"Sarah you need to leaves us alone," I angrily spoke, "We cannot divulge any more information to you."

"Well everyone wants to know so I have to ask the questions," Sarah spluttered back. "Yes, but we have told you the interview is over and now you need to leave." I shouted back.

I was getting angrier and angrier now, "Sarah you to leave now, for your sake."

"We need to leave now guys," I looked away from Sarah and at everyone else, but they were ahead of me. Jetpacks were already on.

I turned everyone invisible, "To Paul's we go. They can't follow us now."

As we flew to Paul's, I calmed down which was good for everyone else.

Chapter 4 : The History of the ISA

"Hey Paul," we all said as we walked into his lair. He was shocked to see us. "Why are you here? What happened to help the town re-build itself?"

"Well, we were helping and the RTÉ news showed. The asked a couple of questions," Molly spoke up, "And then tried to question Peter and ask questions we couldn't answer without risking everything, Jackie was starting to lose the plot, so we left to keep the town safe."

"As well as the news reporter from Jackie," Alice chimed in which made everone including myself laugh.

Irish Spy Agency (ISA) Chronicles Book 2: Chain Retrieval

"Yes, Jackie got pretty angry," Denny spoke, "If we didn't leave, the reporter was going to be injured."

"I would never have hurt her," I said as we all laughed, "I just wanted her to think I would have hurt her so she would back off."

We continued laughing until Paul stopped. "You guys want to go find the next chain or you just want stay here out of the public eye?"

"The latter," I said, "We do have to come with a plan for the other chains without Daniel and the goons showing up to stop us."

"Any board games or things to keep us occupied Paul?" Denny asked.

"I have a better idea," I interrupted, "A lot has happened since I started a few weeks ago with the ISA, and I still don't know the full history and everything that goes with working for the ISA.

"Can you tell me everything? Including how we get our powers or where they come from. How does anyone get chosen. Things like that."

"Let's get started then," Paul stated, "All the way back to the beginning." We all sat down on offices chair around a table which appeared out of nowhere when Paul finished speaking.

In front of me on the table was a notebook and a couple of pens. Both pens had four ink colours in one. One pen had red, black, green, and blue ink and the other had pink, purple, turquoise and lime green.

Irish Spy Agency (ISA) Chronicles Book 2: Chain Retrieval

My obsessive need to have everything in different colours is known by all. I chuckled to myself.

"Well you did hear that the Irish Spy Agency was created by Dean and Diana O'Brien back two thousand years ago," Paul asked, and I nodded.

"They were both scientist and were working on different formulas," Paul started, "No-one actually knows what the formulas were for because like most scientists they kept it all quiet."

"They did experiment on themselves only," Denny announced, "They wanted to keep whatever they discovered to themselves. Until one day they created a formula that gave themselves superpowers."

I tried to keep up with all my notes, but the pens decided to take the notes for me. Great for me, I can listen instead of having to take notes.

"When they discovered their powers," Molly began, "They starting to use them on the competition. Dean had the power of invisibility, but Diana received every power. It took a while before they discovered all her powers."

"The first power she discovered was the same as Alice, Mental manipulation," Jaden said, "They would get Dean to turn them invisible and Diana would manipulated their competition into giving them their scientific findings."

"Diana eventually had enough of that and wanted to help others with the gifts they got,"

Rachel included, "When she sat Dean down they decided to start the Irish Spy Agency. Each person chosen to join them would get this formula injected into them and they receive a power."

"Each person would receive one power. Each generation they would be one person who take over training of the next generation would have all the powers like Diana," Alice said, "She did freak out though every time she discovered a new power.

"They trained new agents all the time in their powers, but they had to hire a fighter to help train them unless they already had the belts in Karate or Tae Won Do or whatever."

"When Diana discovered the power to fly, she loved to fly to clear her head, just like I do," Molly announced, "She was out flying one day when she discovered an Island floating in the sky. Diana had a love of weird, sounding names so she named the island Carabalk Isle."

"As soon as she got back to the agency, she told Dean and the other agents," Nick spoke up this time, "When she brought them to where she found the Island, it was gone. They never believed her. Diana spent years trying to find it.

"Unknown to Dean, Diana had discovered a power that stopped her from aging, and she could also stop those around her from aging as well."

"They spent almost one hundred and ten years searching for the Island," Mike said, "Dean and

Irish Spy Agency (ISA) Chronicles Book 2: Chain Retrieval

Diana were both one hundred and sixty when they re-discovered Carabalk Isle."

"In those years they were searching for the island, they created nine chains that would amplify some of the powers they created," Peter announced, "They gave them to their closest friends and the agency's best agents.

"Dean was one of them, but Diana was not allowed one even though she was the best agent in all the ISA because of all the powers she had."

"Diana did get her hands on the chains though," Nick said, "The agents who got the chains went insane with power. They tried to take over the world and nearly succeeded if Diana didn't take the chains off them without them knowing.

"Something incredible happened when Diana touched the chains though," Peter stated, "As Diana held onto all nine chains, they combined into one, with an all infinity pendant in place of the other pendants."

"Diana sat Dean down and explained to him the they needed to get rid of the chains," Paul interjected, "She told him they were too dangerous. Even in the hands of the agency's most trusted agents.

"Dean agreed instantly, so they spent months trying to destroy the chains. They told no-one so they wouldn't be stopped.

Irish Spy Agency (ISA) Chronicles Book 2: Chain Retrieval

"They hit a problem with destroying the chains though. Diana used every power she had as well as hydrochloric acid and hydrofluoric acid but nothing worked."

"They were getting frustrated," Molly stated, "No matter what they tried, they couldn't destroy the chains. They spent years trying to destroy them, but nothing ever worked.

"Diana came up with a solution to separate them. Because they couldn't destroy them, they would scatter them across the earth to keep them from being used together to destroy the world again."

This was so interesting to learn where the ISA came from and where the powers came from. The two sets of pens were writing so fast I couldn't look at them. "How did we all get our powers then?" I questioned.

"That's part of the story Jackie," Paul stated, "Stop trying to skip ahead. Dean and Diana spent years spreading the chains all over the earth and he moon. But they struggled to find a place for the flight chain, but they knew it had to be somewhere that even with the map nobody would find it.

"Diana knew exactly where she wanted to leave but she just had to find it first. Carabalk Isle. Every time she went flying, she would bring the chain with her."

"When Diana and Dean both turned one hundred and sixty, she found the island again, so she flew to the centre and buried it in the very centre of the island," Molly spoke, "This island is supposed to be filled with so many animals that are supposed to be extinct."

"When Dean and Diana passed away at the age of hundred and seventy-five and the ISA was handed to the next generation, the rules started to change," Peter announced, "Only certain people were allowed to join the agency.

"The new generation got rid of the tak won do, karate trainers because they thought it was a waste of time of the powers we had been given. The people these chose were people who should never have been agents in the first place."

"It took about four hundred years for this to change back to the way Dean and Diana had things," Denny said, "People were chosen by their ability to pick things up extremely fast but also can keep everything a secret.

"Only the parents of the chosen agents were in the know how. Camp duo was discovered by the ISA about three hundred years later but Connor, who used his powers to hide it to the public. Well you've seen what we do there so."

"Connor continued on Dean and Diana legacy," Rachel said, "He continued to choose people they way they did. But he was also able to predict which power they were going to have before the agents were given the powers. Regardless of being able to tell the future.

"Just like Dean and Diana, Connor only trusted a handful of agents. They were all able to predict who was going to get what power based on them watching the future agents life and getting to know them without the person knowing until it was time for them to join."

"Connor was usually the last to predict what power the person was going to have," Mike began, "Each person's power came from within them. The formula that Dean and Diana came with doesn't actually give powers."

"Yes shocker we know," he continued as I was very shocked, "Connor actually discovered our powers were already inside of us, but had no way out. The formula that was injected into us brought the powers out of us more easily."

"Take myself for example," Denny spoke up, "I was always a hothead. I had a bad temper when someone hurt me so I my power was obviously going to be the ability to manipulate fire until Daniel came along and showed me how to create it."

"I'm quite similar to Denny," Rachel explained, "But the difference between us, I can control my temper until my limit. So I got water."

"Peter likes to take on the weight of the world on his shoulders," Molly joked, "He got super strength."

Irish Spy Agency (ISA) Chronicles Book 2: Chain Retrieval

"And Molly is an airhead, that's why she got the power of flight. Her head is always in the clouds," Peter laughed as well as everyone else including Molly.

"Actually I was never told by the ISA why I received the power of flight," Molly explained, "Not that I mind, I can fly without a jetpack." Molly laughed herself this time.

"I have always loved being in nature," Jaden spoke up, "Surrounded by trees, birds and all the other animals has always brought me peace and quiet. I love it so much. I knew my power was either going to be earth or able to communicate or control animals."

"Compared to all these guys," Mike said, "I've never let anyone get under my skin at all but if you mess with my family and friends, I can be worse than Denny or Rachel. I control the air.

"You will know if I ever lose the plot. I can suck the air out of the room or make a hurricane force wind to attack instantly. No need for me to go slow."

"I've perfected the art of manipulation," Alice admitted, "Getting people to do what I wanted them to do without them even knowing I was, was incredible but I eventually learned how to use it for good."

"I'm always trying to be in many places at once," Nick stated, "Wanted to help more people than I could made my life difficult. So I fell in love with my power of duplication because I can be everywhere at once."

"Molly, you could have actually had all the powers," Paul stated, "I saw all your test results from Camp Duo. Molly, you showed the best result in every test given. You could have been Daniel."

"What?" Molly exclaimed, "Why would say that?"

"You are so level-headed and are more carefree than any other soul on the planet, including Daniel," Paul explained, "It was always going to be a toss-up between you and Daniel on who got all the powers. Daniel received them due to his father being the one before him."

"That explains a lot actually," Peter said, "Molly I've always thought we held you back from excelling to be the best version of yourself. But then again, you would never leave us, even if you were commanded."

Everyone laughed again including Molly. "That is me down to a tee," Molly testified, "I could never leave you guys. If I did, the amount of times the ISA would call me to come and clean up after you all. They would be paying me to follow you around 24/7."

Fits of laughter was all we could hear then from everyone. "This brings us full circle back to you Jackie," Paul continued, "The very reason you got the power of invisibility.

Irish Spy Agency (ISA) Chronicles Book 2: Chain Retrieval

"You always felt like you were invisible to everyone around you except your parents," I nodded in agreement, "But that was actually your biggest strength."

"Wh..wh..what?" I stuttered, "How could being invisible be a strength?" There was a moment of silence as I waited for someone to answer.

"Well, you followed these guys here without being caught until you walked in here," Paul answered, "The only people who get through that barrier up there are agents of the ISA or people who are supposed to be a part of the agency. You were always going to be an agent, but it took until you landed here.

"Other than your parents, no-one ever saw you, Jackie. You were even invisible to the ISA. That is an awesome power to have especially when you work at a spy agency. This is why you got the power of invisibility."

"Who knew I would actually be wanted," I suddenly said, "I've never been chosen for anything in my life. Always left until the end of team games and if there was an odd number of people I was never playing." I was almost in tears.

"Now you got us now," Peter insisted, "We are not going anywhere, anytime soon."

"Hear, hear," Everyone else chimed in. It was amazing to see that I was finally wanted.

"There you go Jackie," Paul stated, "You have the entire history of the ISA. Well a summed up

Irish Spy Agency (ISA) Chronicles Book 2: Chain Retrieval

version of it anyway. The Camp Duo lecturer take years to teach everyone."

We all looked at each other and Paul not understanded what he was saying.

"I was in charge of Camp Duo before I was placed in charge of you all. Daniel's dad David was my partner in crime as they say. It was his idea to place you all under my care.

"I loved running Camp Duo but when I was given this team, it was a dream come through after my accident." We all looked at him shocked.

"A story for another time," Paul stated, "Now Jackie is there anything you else you want to know or need to know about the ISA?"

"Yes," I answered, "One question. How does Camp Duo work? I mean like how does it work with the powers and things?"

"Well that remains a mystery today to any of us," Denny said, "No-one alive in the ISA knows the answer to that question."

"That's all for now," I said as I picked up all the notes that was taken for me.

"Any questions you have Jackie," Paul started, "Feel free to ask anyone of us. Now I have to get back to searching for Carabalk Isle."

"Actually Paul," Peter said as he looked at everyone, who nodded back at him with smiles on their faces, "There is one other bit of business we need to take care that only you can agree to."

Irish Spy Agency (ISA) Chronicles Book 2: Chain Retrieval

"What can I do to help? Paul questioned, looking as confused as me.

"Well Paul," Molly started, "We have been chatting and we all decided that Alice is right in her thinking about Jackie."

I was starting to get a bit worried here, "Right about what? Paul and I asked.

"We all decided that I'm stepping down as leader," Peter stated, "Before you start, this has nothing to do with me and what has happened over the last few weeks.

"It's all about you Jackie and the leadership knowledge you have shown in my absence and now Daniel's absence."

"You seemed to know what to do in every situation we find ourselves in," Molly chimed in, "Like finding Peter and the plan to get him back."

"And the map in Australia," Peter continued, "You are always the level-headed one in dangerous situations so we all decided the other night that Alice was right. You belong here as one of us.

"But not s just one of us. Jackie you belong here as the person in charge. We all know Daniel feels the same, whether he remembers or not."

"Daniel was actually the first one to suggest you taking over," Denny joined, "He said he saw a big future a head for you in the ISA, but you had to choose it."

Irish Spy Agency (ISA) Chronicles Book 2: Chain Retrieval

"So Jackie, I'm stepping down as the leader of this team," Peter started, "Are you willing to take my place?"

I was still in shock when I answered, "Why me?" I asked, "Molly is your beta. Why not let her take over for you?"

"Yes, we all know Peter's the Alpha and I'm the beta," Molly answered, "But we both want you to take over as the alpha and then Daniel will be your beta when we get him back."

"This makes the perfect sense for us all," Peter continued, "You and Daniel don't know us all that well, but everything will work better if you are both in charged because we all know each other too well."

"Jackie," Molly started, "On behalf of this team, Will you take over as the leader?"

"Can I think about?" I asked, "I don't think I could make this decision now. Is that alright?"

Everyone fell silent as they all stared at me. All the mouths hung opened in surprise. I really think that they think that I will say no. I burst into laughter.

"As hard as it will to make all the decisions," I started, "Of course I will take over as Alpha, but on one condition."

"What's the condition?" Peter and Molly asked.

"I want you two be the beta's until we get Daniel back."

"Of course, we will," they both answered, "We wouldn't have it any other way."

"What's the first order of business from the new boss?" Denny questioned as everyone burst out laughter.

"I think my order of business as the leader is," I answered, "Denny, I'm benching you!" The look of disgust on her face made laugh even harder. "I'm kidding," I said, "I think we need to head home and go to bed. We can come back here in the morning and discuss where we are going."

"Until tomorrow then Jackie," Paul said, "Everyone get a goodnight sleep and we shall be right back at it tomorrow."

We all shouted goodbye Paul as we let the lair and flew home.

"Be here at nine sharp in the morning," I ordered, "We shall get an early start to the day."

"Look the power of leadership has already gone to her head," Rachel laughed as everyone joined in.

With a goodbye from everyone to everyone, we headed home.

My parents were already eating dinner when I walked into the kitchen. "That smell delicious," I said as I entered.

"Well we are celebrating tonight," My dad said, "Paul rang us after y'all left and he told us the good news."

As I reached the table they both stood up and hugged me.

Irish Spy Agency (ISA) Chronicles Book 2: Chain Retrieval

"I finally got chosen for something that I wasn't force upon. It's incredible," I said with tears in my eyes. My parents were crying as well when I looked up at them.

We stood like that for what felt like forever, but it was only a couple of minutes.

I never noticed what food was on the table until I sat down.

"Dad you did not need to cook this for me," I spoke, "but I do love my truffle chicken with potato gratin."

"As I said , we are celebrating," my dad answered, "You're favourite desert is in the fridge as well."

"No way, you didn't make cheesecake?" I asked shocked as he nodded.

As we all sat down to eat I asked, "How was the rest of the day without us?"

"RTÉ news left not long after you all did when they realised they were getting nothing of us. Most of the town is rebuilt thanks to Nick being there to help."

"It does help to have the power of duplication," I laughed, "Oh I found out a lot about the ISA today when we went back to Paul's."

"Oh what did you find out?" they both questioned at the same time.

"Everyone told me about who started the ISA and how we got our powers," I started, "Nick got the power of duplication due to him wanting to be everywhere at once.

"For me it was because I was invisible to everyone else," my mother reached to touch my arm, "Don't worry, I know now that being invisible is a strength not weakness.

"Working for the ISA we have to be invisible to everyone around us so we can get our missions completed. Now with that I have to head to bed. Big day tomorrow. First day as leader, have to get a good night sleep."

I kissed my parents goodnight and thanked my father again for the food as I headed upstairs to bed.

Chapter 5: Irish Spy Agency Official Training

I woke up so refreshed and ready to take on my first day as leader. As I checked the time on my phone, I realised I never set an alarm. Shoot, I'm going to so late if I don't move now.

At half eight, I had thirty minutes to get a shower and eat breakfast before meeting the gang. A cold shower is all I'm going to have this morning. It takes ages for the shower to heat up and as leader I can't be late.

A cold shower and a couple of cereal bars for breakfast. I needed to be waiting on my team this morning.

Irish Spy Agency (ISA) Chronicles Book 2: Chain Retrieval

I did turn invisible while I waiting on them to show up. I thought it would be fun to have them 'waiting on me to show up.'

As I waited, they took their time showing up. Jaden and Mike were ten minutes early, Alice and Nick were eight minutes early. I sat in silence while they chatted away.

Peter and Rachel arrived at nine on the dot while Molly and Denny hadn't shown up yet. Oh there were going to be in trouble.

Six minutes later they both showed up. "Everyone ready to go?" Molly asked. "Not yet, Jackie's not here yet."

"Boo," I screamed as I turned visible again. They were all terrified except Alice. I knew she would know I was here. "I've been here for like thirty minutes." I said in between laughing.

As I stopped laughing, "I wanted to be here early today to wait on you guys. And then I thought it would be fun to scare you all." I laughed again

"Now it's time to leave," I said as we got our jetpacks on. As we flew to Paul's lair we noticed there was an extra couple of cars in the carpark.

"I wonder who they belong too," Molly asked. "Some ISA big wigs, I guess." Alice answered as we dropped into the castle to Paul's lair.

Alice was right as soon as we entered the main room, Paul was talking to Daniel's father and a couple of other people.

Irish Spy Agency (ISA) Chronicles Book 2: Chain Retrieval

"Good morning all," we all said as we walk in. They were all looking at me including my friends. I think they know who these people are.

"Oh Jackie," David said as he shook my hand, "Congrats on the promotion ."

"Thank you David," I answered blushing. In the background I could hear a woohoo from the gang.

"There is another reason we are here for," David started, "It is time for you to get your driver's license which acts as your company I.D." He continued as he showed me his I.D.

The I.D's are incredible. The original I.D. states David O'Rourke Irish Spy Agency but as he continued to speak and say different companies like An Gardaí Siochana, detective for the Gardaí, IBI, FBI, CIA and even the secret service, Irish Spy Agency changed to each company name. This is when his real eyes change colour and he smirked.

I let it pass because I assumed it was due to the shock of having to take my driver's test. "I'm not ready," I spoke up, "I've not even studied for the theory test yet.

"Ah Jackie," David announced, "We at the Irish Spy Agency do the driving test a little different than the normal driving test for everyone else."

"We will be heading to Camp Duo soon," the lady said, "We just need to hear about what is happening with trying to find Daniel first."

"Well," I began, and Paul looked at me and nodded his head. So now I have to be careful of

Irish Spy Agency (ISA) Chronicles Book 2: Chain Retrieval

what I say, "We have found him a couple of times but when we get there. There is too many goons around him to get him back. Then Daniel and goons attack us."

"He attack his team," The lady spoke, "Are we going to have a repeat of what happened to Peter?"

"No you see," I began, "What happened to Peter is very different, he was brainwashed. Daniel got retrograde amnesia in the battle at the school and the enemy convinced him we are the enemy and not the other way around."

"That's good to know Jackie," David said, "I know we have the best team on the job and unless Mark takes you off the job or gives you another job."

"Anyway," The Lady spoke up, "That's great news. But now it's time to go to Camp Duo. Jackie are you ready?"

"Not really," I said, "But let's go." Taking the ladies hand as David took her other hand and the man placed his hand on her shoulder. And we disappeared.

We appeared in the same field as we always do. "Now Jackie," David stated, "It's not just your driver's test today. It's your official ISA test. The drivers test is for your I.D., but the rest of the test is for you to stay in ISA. And before you ask the rest of the test are mandatory."

I didn't know what to do so I just nodded. "Do you have any questions?" The lady asked.

"What tests do I have to do?" I asked. "You have to fight hand to hand, with every type of weapon, drive a vehicle and then we run test on your power of invisibility," David told me.

"Is it in that order? Or what happens first?" I questioned. "Everything happens in that order because it takes a while normally for powers to manifest in the person." The lady answered.

"Let's start then," I said, "The quicker we start the faster I can get back to my team."

"Follow me," David said, "We need to start with the hand to hand combat."

As I followed David into the building that the kids ran out, the first time we were here training with Daniel.

Camp Duo is one of the most beautiful places in the world. Even inside was beautifully painted. A safe place for children.

I was brought into a room that had men and women lined up around the wall, a couple of inches apart from each other. I think I counted about fifty altogether.

"The first test is to fight every single one of these people and win," Daniel spoke, "You have to beat more than ninety percent to pass this test though."

Irish Spy Agency (ISA) Chronicles Book 2: Chain Retrieval

"Only problem David," I began, "I've only fought once and that was here for training with Daniel a few weeks ago."

"Channel the spirit you had then Jackie," David started, "If you fail these test unfortunately that's the end your time with the agency."

Something I did not want to think about was having to leave the agency as I have to complete the training to stay. I got to do this for me and for my team.

David handed me a bag and said, "You can change in the room over there." I walk towards the room, he pointed out.

I changed as fast as I could into a light t shirt and running pants. Both were navy coloured.

I was debating with myself whether or not to go out there because I was dreading fighting anyone but for the team I took a deep breath and left the changing room and walked to the middle of the room.

David came over to me and placed one of the bracelets on my hand, "To stop you using your power," he said, and I nodded. Daniel had already used these bracelets on us. "Good luck." He said while walking.

Another deep breath as I looked around at this men and women around the room. 'If looks could kill' popped into my head. These men and women were as big as wrestlers so I could definitely lose this fight.

Irish Spy Agency (ISA) Chronicles Book 2: Chain Retrieval

"Are you ready Jackie?" David asked. Closing my eyes to take a deep breath. "Ready," I said getting into my fight stance.

"Attack," David shouted, and everything changed. I was fighting for my life.

I had to get the feeling of dread out of my system. My team popped into my head, and I knew I had to win this.

Without even thinking about it I went into fight mode, my friends were in danger, and they needed me to get to them.

I instantly blocked the two kicks coming at me by flipping backwards. I was surrounded by at least eight of them when I stood up facing them.

Out of nowhere I was able to bounce into the air and kick them all sending them all flying across the room.

Where was all this coming from? I've never been in a fight before except training with Daniel and the team here a few weeks ago.

I forgot what I was doing and was sent flying across the room myself.

Standing up to shake it off. I noticed two of the women sent me flying.

"Enough," I screamed. Within five minutes all of the men and women were lying on floor unconscious.

As I was catching my breath, David came over and shook my hand. "Jackie, you just beat the

Irish Spy Agency (ISA) Chronicles Book 2: Chain Retrieval

agency's record. This is normally the longest part of the ISA tests. Even your team didn't finish this fast.
"On to the weaponry tests now. This way." We left that room and into the next one.
This room had a boing man dummy set up in here.
"What happens in here?" I questioned. "Well in here you will be tested on a few types of weapons from daggers to bo staffs to swords and everything in between."
"Great, sounds like a lot of fun," I answered.
"First up are Shuriken," David spoke. "What are they?" I asked confused. "Ninja death stars," he answered.
I shivered, those sound very dangerous. I walks a women carrying a tray of what I guessed was the ninja death stars. Metal stars with extremely sharp edges.
"The test here is to throw the shuriken at the targets but you have to missed the human who will be doing flips and jumps in front of them."
"You want me to hit those targets while a human prances around in front of them. Won't that killed them if I hit them with it?"
"The only people going to be in front of you is the agents with power of healing," David said, "It's safe to hit them." He laughed.
I picked up one of the shuriken, they were so light for a weapon of destruction. "Begin," David shouted.

Irish Spy Agency (ISA) Chronicles Book 2: Chain Retrieval

When I looked up, a man and women were jumping around and flipping in front of the targets.

Taking a deep breath, I picked up a few more Shuriken and threw them one by one at the target.

Not wanting to look up, I was terrified I hit the both of them, but I heard cheering coming from the targets.

"What happened? Who did I hurt?" I questioned absolutely terrified.

"You did something that took every other agent a long time to master," David said as he chuckled, "No one is hurt but you pinned the two agents to the targets with shuriken."

Not wanting to look but David couldn't stop chuckling in front of me. I glanced up and saw the man and woman pinned to the targets.

"I did that?" I was so confused. I've never did anything like this before. "Yes Jackie," David answered, "This was all you."

Still in shock, I took a deep breath. "Are you ready to move on Jackie?" "Where to next?"

"We are going back into the first room for the next five weaponry tests: Daggers, Sais, Nun Chucks, Bo Staff, and Katana. There are too many weapons to test you on, so we pick different size weapons to test instead."

"Great," I started, "I hate holding a butter knife." I starting giggling myself this time. "Your test is to defeat each of them. You have nothing to worry

Irish Spy Agency (ISA) Chronicles Book 2: Chain Retrieval

about Jackie," David stated, "You are a natural. Daniel had the best scores up until now.

"Paul was right when he told me you were born to be in this agency."

As we re-entered the room, I noticed a few men and women were here holding the different weapons I have to fight with.

"Now Jackie," David began, "These people are the best in the world for each of their chosen weapons.

"You will start with the daggers," David continued, "Then unto the duo sais, nun chucks, Bo staff, and finally the katana sword."

"I look forward the Bo staff, the least violent of them all." I laughed.

"Jackie, you are a natural," David said, "You belong in the ISA. No need to be worrying about anything."

A man stepped forward with two daggers in his hands, so I stepped forward and picked up two the daggers on the table.

I took a deep breath and stood in front of the man. In a fight stance, one in front of me and the other over my head. "É a thabhairt ar an bhfear." (Bring it on man.)

As the man attack me, I bent my knees and pushed up. I flipped over him and poked in the back with the dagger.

I smirked thinking I was winning when he turned around so fast and knocked the dagger poking his back to the ground and pointed one of his to my neck.

Taking a deep breath, I bent down and kicked his foot from under him. As he fell backwards I ran over and picked up my dagger and fought back.

The four daggers clashed against each other as we kicked each other as well. A picture of my team popped into my head, and I stabbed the man by accident, and he collapsed.

Everyone around started clapping. Finally this test was over.

Now time for the duo sais. Only ever seen these in films, I didn't know much about them. For those who have never heard of them, they are like a three pronged fork.

The two outside prongs are normally between two and three inches long while the middle prong is between five and eight inches long.

As I picked them up, the middle prong went on the inside of my arms, and I stood in my fighting stance with them. Two women came out and stood in front of me.

The sais clashed against each other as we fought. I'm starting to really enjoy myself at this stage. I fought for my team, so I was kicking the two women's backside.

I did jump up and kick the two women at the same time sending them flying. When they both got back up, I had my sais on both their necks.

Irish Spy Agency (ISA) Chronicles Book 2: Chain Retrieval

"Time for nun chucks," David announced, "Jackie you are a natural. I have to admit, I think you do belong here at the ISA."

Two men replaced the two women each with two nun chucks. I placed the duo sais on the table and picked up the nun chucks. A weapon I know I would fail.

The men were swinging them around like there were nothing while I was struggling to swing them around without hitting myself. "Can we move on?" I asked while hitting myself in the arm again.

Everyone was laughing at me. "Moving on," David said staring at me. I heard something really weird as I was heading to put the nun chucks on the table.

No one else notice so I thought I was hearing things. But when I focused on the sound, I could see them.

Multiple shuriken were coming for me, but they were invisible. Even with the bracelet on me stopping my power, I could still see them. I forgot Daniel told us that our powers would work even when we can't use them help protect us from danger.

As I stopped the shuriken hitting me, I was trying to figure out who threw them at me. David was the only one not looking at me.

Irish Spy Agency (ISA) Chronicles Book 2: Chain Retrieval

I knew something was wrong with David. I needed to talk to Alice about this when I get back. Until then I'll continue to train and pass these tests.

Picking up the bo staff, I ran my hand along it. This is the one weapon I know how to use. Swinging it round diagonally, I stopped it halfway up back with my arm straight out the side.

This one was going to be so much fun. I was surround by men and women with other bo staffs. They attack and the sound of wood hitting wood could be heard at the other end of the building.

As we were fighting three of them hit my bo staff, it broke down the middle. I could hear David speak to the other lady giving the tests, that I failed this part of the test.

"No, it's not David," I screamed, "I fought with a bo staff before I know how to use it, even when it splits down the middle."

I ran towards to the group and attacked, within thirty seconds, they were all down.

Hearing shocked gasps around me, I took a bow. "Now, what's next?" "The last weaponry test is a katana sword."

Picking up the katana sword after I placed the bo staff down. This fight is going to be the worse fight of them all. This will be for my team.

"Now Jackie, this is the second last test," David announced, "After this is power fighting but we have already see how powerful you're invisibility

Irish Spy Agency (ISA) Chronicles Book 2: Chain Retrieval

powers are, so we are going from here unto the driving test."

As terrified as I was to fight with a sword in my hand, I knew I had to prove to David and everyone here that I belong in the ISA.

I had one sword but there was three others against me. Two men and a woman. All three attack but as I jumped backwards, I hit the other swords with mine.

This fight was petrifying but for my team, I would win. We fought for what seemed like forever, but five minutes had passed.

I was slashing the sword from left to right to keep the men and the lady away from me. I was hitting the other swords at some points to.

Fighting hand to hand as well as with a sword was difficult to say the least. But I was finally getting the hang of it. I was going to win this fight for me and my team.

I focused on the three people in front of me. And I charged at them. Jumping into the air kicking the woman down and then the man. I slashed the last woman with the sword, from shoulder to waist.

There was no blood though, cables appeared instead. It was a set-up there was no real people fighting me. I'm so happy there was no one really hurt.

Irish Spy Agency (ISA) Chronicles Book 2: Chain Retrieval

"Well done Jackie," David stated, "You flew through all these tests. Passing Daniel's times by hours. He was the top agent until now."

"I'm glad that that's finished," I spoke up, "But I'm happy I did it."

"Until to the final test now before we head back to Paul's," David said, "Driving test."

I shuddered, I had forgotten about the driving test. The test I had actually come here for.

"Follow us," the lady sad as her and David walked outside. Outside there was a car, one of the fanciest cars I've ever seen.

A purple Bugatti Chiron Super Sport was waiting for me. "Last test before we head for back to Paul's. And fill the team in on how you did."

I slid into the driver seat and pulled on my seatbelt. "Where is the driving course?" I questioned the instructor sitting beside me.

"That's actually for you to tell me, Ms Sprint," the instructor answered, "The course is set for each agents power."

"Oh that seams cool," I said as I closed my eyes and took a deep breath, and looked up. "I see it now."

"Start whenever you would like," she said. Taking another deep breath, I turned the car on.

All I know about cars are the pedal are clutch on the inside, brake in the middle and accelerate on the outside but there is only two pedals so I'm

Irish Spy Agency (ISA) Chronicles Book 2: Chain Retrieval

guessing that there is only a brake and accelerate pedals.

I put my foot down slowly on the pedal. As I slowly made the car move, I noticed the instructor marked my sheet. I didn't know what was wrote down, so I sped up.

Still so nervous but speeding up, none the less. I drove so fast through the course, up hills around bends, overtaking other vehicles. In ten minutes I was finished.

David and the lady we arrived with were still standing where I left them, waiting on me.

Stepping out of the car David spoke to me, "We have good news and bad news Jackie. Which would you like first?"

"The bad news please," I answered. "Well the bad news is you can never fight with nun chucks," he said laughing, "This was the only part of the test you failed."

"And the good news?" I quizzed them. "The good news is here is your company I.D." the lady answered, "You passed everything else. Now hold on, I'm sending you back to Paul's."

Arriving back in Paul's lair, I was so happy to be officially part of the ISA. That feeling disappear as soon as I arrived in Paul's lair and was replaced with the feeling of dread.

Everyone was lying on beds, covered in blood and bandages, groaning in pain.

"What the hell happened to you all?" I screamed, "I was gone for like four hours," I had to check my watch to see the time.

"Jackie, " Paul began, "I tried healing them, but nothing has worked."

"Tell me everything," I shouted. "You better sit down," Paul stated, "It's a long story as a chair appeared for me to sit down.

Chapter 6: My Team

Paul started pacing the floor at this point as David and the Lady left. . "Paul will you just tell me what happened to my team when I was not here?" I screamed at him.
"I don't know where to begin," he answered.
"Stop pacing and just start at the beginning," I said. A chair appeared for Paul to sit down.
"When you left this morning, I gave the team a day off with no research and no travel while you doing all those tests for the ISA and they were attacked," he began, "Daniel and the goons attacked out of nowhere and left them all for dead."

Irish Spy Agency (ISA) Chronicles Book 2: Chain Retrieval

"Where did they go?" I asked. "They went to Courtown to play mini golf at Pirates Cove. He surprised them so they didn't have a chance to fight back. They were left for dead."

"How did you get them back here?" "Alice can astral project herself across the world. But obviously she was injured so her power did it for her. She told me they needed help. I got there just in time but the guards were already there.

"I had to show them my badge and I took over the scene. I was able to duplicate myself and drive them all back here while I stayed at the scene. I told the guards my twin was taking them all to the hospital.

"When I got back here, I tried healing them all one by one, but nothing is working so I tried bandaging up the wounds, but the bleeding won't stop."

I was listening to it all and gasping, "Maybe Daniel did something that would keep them down while they searched for the other chains."

"That's the other thing," he stated, "Daniel took the chains off Rachel and Denny."

"No way," I screamed, "Firstly, we will get them back. Secondly I will head to pirate's cove now and look for some clues and you will stay here and keep trying to heal them."

"You don't have company I.D. yet," Paul stated, "So I have to go and look for clues."

Irish Spy Agency (ISA) Chronicles Book 2: Chain Retrieval

"Well Paul about that," I looked at him, "I passed all but one test at Camp Duo. I didn't have to do the power test, but I failed the nun chucks." I said as I showed him my very own company I.D.

"I was not planning on going like this any way," I stated, "I was going to turn invisible and go look around without anyone knowing."

"I'll call the guards watching the place and let them know my colleague is coming down to have a look around as I haven't had a chance yet," Paul said, "Be careful while you do. Make sure you are listening to everything around you."

"Paul don't worry about me," I started, "I'm not going alone. I am going to get Bonnie and Geoffrey to come with me." He sighed happy as I was walking away.

Outside in the carpark, there was a motorbike with a bow on it and helmet waiting for me. Throwing my leg over the bike to sit down, I opened my phone to ring my mother and see if she could get in touch with Bonnie and Geoffrey for me.

As I scrolled down my contacts to get down to my mother, I passed Bonnie's number. Whoops I forgot the gang put their parents numbers in my phone in case I couldn't get the team.

I called Bonnie. It rang twice when she picked up, *"Detective Brown, how can I help?"*

"Hey Bonnie, it's Jackie. I was wondering if you and Geoffrey could meet me at the Pirate's Cove. I need to see the scene." "What happened at Pirate's Cove, Jackie?"

"I thought Paul would have told you all. But it's important you both meet me there. I'll tell you everything when we get there, I promise." "Of course Jackie, we'll meet you there."

I hung up. "Paul, I know it's been tough," I said into the watch, "But you need to tell the gangs parents so they can be here for them. Let my parents come too but let them I know I'm safe.

"Bonnie and Geoffrey are coming with me, so I'll let them know. Wish me luck." "Good Luck Jackie, I'll ring them now."

It was fun driving the car at Camp Duo, but this was a motorbike. Taking a deep breath, I turned the key in the ignition. It roared to life.

Placing the helmet on my head ad throwing the visor down, I drove down the lane as fast as I could. Driving out past castle garden's nursing home heading for the new M11. I needed to get to Pirate's Cove as fast as I could.

Zooming in and around the cars I was approaching twice the speed, but I didn't care. My team needed me to do this for them.

Normally taking thirty minutes to get to Courtown, it took me ten minutes. Jumping off my bike as I parked it. Bonnie and Geoffrey were waiting for me. "Jackie, tell us what happened?" they both questioned me.

Irish Spy Agency (ISA) Chronicles Book 2: Chain Retrieval

"Well I wasn't around so I don't actually know but Paul said the guys were attack here while having a day off. I was away with the ISA doing the official training.

"So it's my job now to find out what happened, and I need both of your help. Yes I know you both want to be back with your kids, but Paul called everyone else to go and be with them. Including my parents so I need you both here."

They both nodded in agreement while we approached the yellow tape we were stopped by the guards.

"P.I Jackie Sprint and these are Detective Brown and Detective O'Leary. My colleague P.I. O'Rourke rang and said we were coming."

The two guards just nodded and lifted the tape up and let us pass. An accident to this magnitude has Pirate's cove closed for a few days.

That's great for us as we look around for evidence because no one else will be able to get in.

Heading inside, the manager showed us to where Paul found the agents lying. They hadn't even made it half-way around the course, they got to hole six.

To be honest, I wish I was here with the team, at least we would be going through this together. But I also know the team are happy I wasn't with them. At least they have family on the case.

Irish Spy Agency (ISA) Chronicles Book 2: Chain Retrieval

The three of us started walking around, bending down to see under bushes. We walked around all eighteen holes and found nothing.

"I think I need to go up and have a look around and see if I the height can make a difference," I said to Bonnie and Geoffrey.

They both nodded and continued searching on the ground. A jetpack appeared on my back and up over the crazy golf course I went.

I saw nothing as I flew around. Time to turn invisible and flew around again. This time spotting eight empty vials on the ship.

I waved my hand over them and shouted and Bonnie and Geoffrey, "Head to the ship," as I flew down.

Bonnie and Geoffrey were already there. Bagging the vials. "Can I take them back to Pauls?" I asked them, "You can meet me there. You can be there for the kids."

The nodded, "We will bring these with us as you are on the bike," Bonnie told me. As we were walking out, Geoffrey grabbed my arm, "Jackie, what's that in the water?"

As I looked into the water, it was another vial. "Get some divers over here," Bonnie and Geoffrey shouted.

"I got this," I said as I jump over the railing and dived. The watch help me see where I was going. The vial was different than the others. This one was full and green. Swimming back up Geoffrey was on my side of the railing holding out his hand. Picking me and Bonnie helping us both back on to dry land.

"Jackie, why did you that?" Bonnie asked concerned. "Paul is not sure who we can trust right now, and you too are the only people I would trust on a case. I'm new to all this and Paul was happy with bringing you along.

"We don't actually know who is the goons side right now either, there might be people you work with every day on the goons side. I couldn't risk the diver tampering with the evidence."

Heading back to the car and the motorbike, "Jackie you need to dry off before we drive back," Geoffrey said. Just a concerning parent.

"I'm going to sit I your car before we go, and the watch is going to completely dry me off. Before I head back on the bike."

I climbed into the car and the watch, filled the car with hot air and within seconds I was bone dry. Cooling down the car before I stepped out.

"Now we head back to Paul's," I spoke to Geoffrey and Bonnie, "I follow behind you on the bike and together we'll make sure these vials get back to Paul."

Jumping on the bike and driving behind or beside the car. It was slower going back but I had to make sure the vials would get back to Paul.

Along the M11 there was a problem though. Traffic slowed down to a standstill. Something was definitely wrong. I tapped on Bonnie's window.

Irish Spy Agency (ISA) Chronicles Book 2: Chain Retrieval

"I'm going to drive up and see what's happening." Driving on ahead. Something was off. There was nothing blocking the road.

Focusing more on the start of the traffic jam. There was an invisible force field stopping the cars from moving.

I need to focus on my power more often so I can learn to see invisible things instantly. "Paul, I need you on the M11 now." I screamed into the watch as I drove back to Bonnie and Geoffrey.

Reaching the car, "This is an ambush," I started as Paul appeared beside me with Alice on another motorbike, "Paul here, is going to take you both straight back to the lair. Alice and I are going to keep going on the bike to distract them."

I didn't even question how Alice was here healed. "Paul, get these out of here and bring those vials with you. Alice lets go have some fun. We'll keep them busy."

Paul took Bonnie and Geoffrey back to the lair. "Alice, I need to talk to you but that will wait as we go have some fun."

Alice nodded as we zoom down towards the force field. I made the force disappear as we drove by to let the traffic continue.

"Congratulation Jackie," Alice said to mind, "Welcome to the ISA officially." We were having so much fun racing down the road together, we never noticed the other motorbikes at first.

Irish Spy Agency (ISA) Chronicles Book 2: Chain Retrieval

Alice sensed them first because she screamed at me, "They're following us Jackie. We can't lead them back to the Lair. The others are not strong enough yet."

We were nearly at Enniscorthy at this time, so we turned off and headed for Bunclody. "Let's head to Bunclody, I've got family there. That will help us until we can get back to Paul," Alice nodded as we drove towards Bunclody.

Speeding down the road to Bunclody, "Alice we gotta stop for petrol, I'm running low." As we driving Alice screamed at me, "Jump on my bike."

"What?" I screamed back in shock. "Yes Jackie, the bike's are like the cars we have it will automatically go back Paul's."

"Here goes nothing," I said as I stood up on the seat of the bike as it was going and pushed jumped off. Landing on the back of Alice's bike I instantly wrapped my arms around here. My bike disappeared.

Still driving down the road. Alice took a right and stopped for moment. "What are you doing?" I questioned.

"Just wait," she whispered, "Lets stretch our legs for a moment." I got off the bike and jumped into the bush. Alice got off and just stood staring at the road we just came off.

"It's fine Jackie," she whispered again, "I've made it look like we drove on. They didn't see us take the right." Just as she finished whispering they drove by so fast.

"We can head back to Paul's now," she said getting on the bike. "Can we chat first?" I asked, Let's go get food in here." We walked across the road to restaurant called Ballycarney Inn.

Sitting down, a waitress came over to take our order. "Hello, my name is Trish," She started, "Can I get you drinks to start with?"

"I actually know what I would like to order," I stated, as Alice nodded in agreement, "Can I have the fish and chips and a coke zero please?" Alice smiled, "Same here thanks." Trish smiled at us as she walked away.

"So, what would you like to chat about?" Alice quizzed. "What I'm about to tell you, I need you promise to keep this from everyone including Nick. Can you do that for me?"

Trish brought our food out at this point, "Well it depends on what you tell me." "Oh well this is so out there, that I myself doesn't think it's really happened?" "In that case Jackie, I'll listen."

"Let's sit in silence and eat," I said, "I need you to read my mind and see what I mean for yourself." As we ate Alice worked her way through my mind.

Alice could see every part of my training and she was smiling and happy for me. When she got to the part about the multiple shuriken coming at me. She was shocked.

Irish Spy Agency (ISA) Chronicles Book 2: Chain Retrieval

She didn't say anything as she moved on. She laughed at me when she got to the nun chucks part. As she continued to go through my memories we sat and ate in silence.

"So what do you need to tell me?" "As you saw multiple shuriken attack me invisible but no one but David knew something had happened.

"I think David still has his powers and is the leader of the bad guys. I didn't want to say anything because he is Paul's best friend, but he is either the leader or he knows who the leader is."

"Jackie, I know are only trying to help but there could be others undercover in the agency," Alice began, "It could have been anyone."

"Think about Alice," I stated, David and the lady were the only two people I was around all day. The lady was the one who transported me Camp Duo and back not David, yet shuriken attacked me.

"I think he plans to take us all out, but I just don't know his plan yet. Promise me you will block this thoughts out of your head until we can figure what is going on with the ISA."

"I promise, but we will need help if we decide to go ahead with this idea about the ISA , we will need help. I will tell Nick what is going on, but our minds have synced up more and more over the years. I can protect all three of minds even when we are separated."

"Thank you," I answered, "I assumed you would think I was crazy and overthinking everything."

Irish Spy Agency (ISA) Chronicles Book 2: Chain Retrieval

"We should head back to Paul's," Alice said standing up, "I'll pay the bill." Alice went over to the bar to pay the bill.

I got up and walked over to the exit while waiting on Alice. "Alice, it's time to go." I shouted across the bar to her. "Keep the change," she said to Trish behind the counter running over to me.

"What's wrong?" she asked. "Daniel's here," I screamed, "We got to go and go now."

"Leave the bike," she said, "This way." I followed her over the bar counter, I saw she nodded at Trish, and we ran out the back through the kitchen.

"We gotta fly back to Paul's as fast as we can," Alice said, "And faster than they can follow." We were halfway through the kitchen when we noticed goons were coming this way too.

"Alice, what are we going to do? We are outnumbered." "Jackie we gotta go back and fight. Trish will help us. She is ISA after all."

Heading back to the bar we could hear Daniel, "Jackie. Alice. I know you are both here. Come out and fight."

"You want us," I screamed as Alice and I jumped over the bar, "Come and get us."

This was going to be fun. "Hey Daniel," I shouted, "Did you hear I beat your score at ISA for the official training." I laughed as goons attacked me.

Irish Spy Agency (ISA) Chronicles Book 2: Chain Retrieval

Kicking there behind right back to Daniel who didn't look happy. I did notice he was wearing Rachel and Denny's chains though.

"Hand to hand combat Daniel," I said looking at him, "No powers. Just our fists and feet." He nodded.

Looking over at Alice, "You take care of the goons." Alice and Trish, who jumped over the bar counter and starting fighting as well. They both kicked the goons ass.

Daniel locked eyes on me. I dragged him outside in an invisible box. "Alice and Trish can fight inside with your goons, while you and I fight out here."

Knowing Daniel but also knowing that Daniel is working for the bad guys now, he won't stick to the no power rule. But all I need to do was the grab the chains off his neck.

"Let's do this," I screamed. Daniel ran for me, but I slid underneath him and tripped him up. "How did you do that?" "You're dad has taught me some tricks since I saw you last."

As he got back up I kicked him in the back and sent him flying across the car park. I need those chains now. Concentrating on his neck, I made an invisible grip hand grip on them and pulled them all the way to me and placed them into my pocket.

"You attacked the wrong people Daniel," I screamed, "Leave now. Or you will regret it."

Out of nowhere a hole appeared in the ground and Daniel fell in but held onto the edge. As much

Irish Spy Agency (ISA) Chronicles Book 2: Chain Retrieval

as he struggled nothing was working for him. He was stuck in the ground.

Looking around to see what was happening. My team was here. "Now you and the goons have no chance. Especially since I have these," I said holding up the chains, "Never attack my team again. Or there will be horrible consequences for you and the goons."

"Let him up Jaden. He's going to leave." Jaden open the floor and Daniel screamed at the goons, "Let's go, now."

They all ran out of the restaurant and flew after Daniel, but they were badly bruised and were bleeding loads. Alice and Trish ran out after them.

"They're gone but looks whose back," I said looking Alice and Trish. But Nick was already at Alice's side.

"Trish, thanks for your help," I said, "Alice and I could not have done this without you today."

"Anytime," Trish answered, "I love working for the ISA. And it's finally nice to work with other members."

"Trish is there anything we can do for you? We can help tidy up inside. We know Alice to well. There is definitely a huge mess inside," I asked. Everyone laughed.

"No need Jackie honestly," Trish told, "I'll have the mess cleaned up in like 30 seconds."

Irish Spy Agency (ISA) Chronicles Book 2: Chain Retrieval

Shaking hands with Trish, "If there is anything we can do, please get in touch with us but for now we need to say goodbye. Thanks."

Trish waved at us as we flew back towards Enniscorthy and unto Paul's lairs.

"What was wrong with you all after?" I quizzed.

"Whatever Daniel injected us with removed the zinc, iron, calcium, and vitamin a, b, and c from our bodies which prevent Paul form being able to heal us," Molly said.

"Alice here though, with her powers she manipulated other vitamins and minerals in her body and turned them into zinc, iron, calcium, and vitamin a, b, and c," Nick said, "As she was going to help us all, you rang for help."

"My bad," I said, "But I'm glad you are all ok. I was really worried when I arrive back from Camp Duo."

"Never apologize for asking for help," Rachel said, "My mother and Mike's father are safe with Paul right now. You did the right thing."

"Congratulations on passing the ISA official test," Peter said, "Did you pass them all?"

"The only test I failed was the nun chucks," I answered, "They skipped the power test because they've already seen me use the power so many times."

"Nun chucks are not my thing either," Denny said, "We all have our weapons of choice based on how natural they all felt in the training." I laughed,

Irish Spy Agency (ISA) Chronicles Book 2: Chain Retrieval

"That's thing, every other weapon felt natural. The daggers, sais, shuriken, bo staff, and the sword were all easy to use and slay people with. But the nun chucks were just not for me."

They all laughed at me, but I knew it wasn't to hurt me so I joined in.

Getting closer to Enniscorthy I noticed the sun was shining. Which rarely happenings in Enniscorthy. But it means one thing and one thing only.

The town is going to be full of people and yes I know they already know who we are and what we do, but they don't know where our base is, so I had to turn everyone invisible.

Flying closer to Vinegar Hill, I noticed our parents cars are still in the carpark, my motorbike is also there with Alice's.

"Why are our parents still here?" I questioned.

"Our parents stayed behind to help Paul tidy up," Peter said, "Remember we were beat up badly and left for dead. There was sweat and blood all over Paul's floor. Paul is sometimes queasy when it comes to blood."

Landing in the lair, we walked into the main room. Paul and our parents were chatting waiting for us.

"Hey," announcing our arrival, "What's happening?"

"Just waiting on you guys to come back," Paul stated, "Now we can celebrate the good news.

Irish Spy Agency (ISA) Chronicles Book 2: Chain Retrieval

Jackie, welcome to the Irish Spy Agency. Officially, you can now boss all these guys around." We all laughed as our parents turned around with a congratulations sign. Everyone screamed in excitement.

"For now we must continue on with the mission," Paul stated, "Jackie, on welcoming you into the agency, we think you should go and find the invisibility chain."

"Well speaking of chains," I said taking out the two in my pocket, "Denny and Rachel, I have something for you both." I handed them both their chains.

"How did you get them?" they both asked.

"Daniel had them on when we were fighting and I took them off him without him noticing."

"This is why you are the boss," Denny screamed putting on the chain.

"Now we can move on Paul," I announced.

Chapter 7: The Sistine Chapel Italy

They were all staring at me. Oh crap, I forgot I had to make the decision on where we go. "Sorry I forgot your waiting on me to make the decision," I said, "Let's go to Italy then. We drive to the airport and fly."

"Best of luck this time," Paul said as we were running out the door, "Fly into Ciampino Airport in Rome."

I ran towards the cars in the carpark but Alice yelled at me, "Bikes this time Jackie."

"Mine is empty remember?" I reminded her, "I can't drive mine."

Irish Spy Agency (ISA) Chronicles Book 2: Chain Retrieval

"Jackie, the tank is full, that's what happens when the return without us," Molly told me, "And we need the bikes for the roads in Rome because we can drive on whatever road we want."

"Yes Jackie," Denny said, "It's the joys of having the ISA company badges." Running and jumping on to my bike as everyone was on theirs.

"Let's go," I said placing the helmet on my head up.

Speeding down the road on to the M11 again. I chuckled to myself. I might build a house on either end because I seem to be on this road more than I'm off it.

"I'm winning," Denny screamed as we drove to the airport.

"It's not a race Denny," I shouted, "But it is now." Speeding down the M11 reaching two hundred kilometres I passed all the cars on the road as my team were way behind me.

I glanced back to see where they were and they were getting closer to me.

"Alice, is there anything happening above?" I asked, "Traffic doesn't just build up like this unless there's accident."

We kept driving towards the airport when we did come across an accident. A four vehicle accident.

Stopping driving the bike, I jump into action. With my mother being the head of neurology, I was first aid trained my entire life.

Irish Spy Agency (ISA) Chronicles Book 2: Chain Retrieval

"Everyone spread out and check the cars," I screamed, "Denny we don't need fire here so go ring 999 for ambulance and the guards. Then ring for Bonnie and Geoffrey and get them here."

Denny did not like that but we don't need any accidental sparks setting a fire or causing an explosion.

I ran towards the upside down pickup truck and without even thinking and dive unto all the glass and underneath.

There was a man moving slowly in the driver's seat and a woman unconscious in the passenger seat. "Sir don't move. We are going to get you both out of here." He didn't move but I knew he understood.

"Two in here," I screamed standing up, "Nick I need you get in there and get him out. You will need help though because he has stopped moving but he still breathing."

Nick went straight to work as I ran around trying to look at the other vehicles. "Jackie, we got these ones, go back to the pickup truck," Molly screamed at me.

I jumped down to check on the women, she was breathing and had a pulse but was still unconscious. "Denny, how far away is the ambulance."

"There nearly here," she said, "Bonnie and Geoffrey are on the way as well, they will take over the scene when they arrive."

Irish Spy Agency (ISA) Chronicles Book 2: Chain Retrieval

"Great Denny," I answered, "Now get over here and help get this lady out." She ran over to me as I got into the pickup truck. Taking the seatbelt off the lady.

With the help of my powers we got her out safe and straight into the recovery position. Looking up the ambulances were here and everyone was out of their vehicles.

"Jackie, what's going on?" Geoffrey questioned. "We came across this accident when we were heading to the airport, " I answered, "We jumped into action and got the people out. It's all we know."

He nodded and went over to Bonnie. We helped get all the people into the ambulances before I said, "Let's get going. We got a mission to complete."

Getting on my bike, I realised they were all looking at me. "What is wrong?" "Our clothes!" they all pointed out.

While I was looking at them our watches changed our clothes for us. At least we won't be stop at the airport now.

"Now we can head to the airport," I said as we laughed and got on to our bikes. We waved goodbye to Bonnie and Geoffrey and drove off towards to the airport.

Leaving the accident behind, we continued our race down the road to the airport. Denny and Molly were in the lead.

Irish Spy Agency (ISA) Chronicles Book 2: Chain Retrieval

Mike pulled into the lead as we pulled into the airport winning the race, Denny was not happy with him at all.

Driving through the airport, I realised it was packed and we had to be stealthier.

I was heading to where we went last time until Rachel said, "Jackie our plane is already for us we just have to head gate 24 this time. We just need to find the entrance we can enter with these without going through security with them."

"Even better," I whispered, "Going through security is the worst thing about the airport."

They were all staring at me. "What? Am I still covered in blood?" I asked while searching over my body looking for blood.

Laughing at me, I was still confused. "You have to find the door for us Jackie, so we can enter with the bikes," Molly told me.

"Oh ok," I answered, "I was confused about why you were looking at me." Looking around the terminal buildings. "What terminal are we going to?" I quizzed, "I found many doors in both terminals."

"Terminal one," Rachel spoke up, "Where are the doors?" "Over there," I pointed, "And there."

"Alice your turn," Molly said, "Which door leads past security?" Alice stared at both doors as she flew towards both.

Looking through the wall of the first door and then she flew towards the other door. Staring in there she waved us all over. "It's this one," She said pointing at the door, "The other leads us directing to security."

I pushed the door opened as I walked through turning everyone invisible as we walked through. "Alice, can you shrink the bikes to keyrings until we get on the plane?" I asked.

"Yes I can," she answered, "But it won't last long so we better get a move on." "Great, everyone into the bathroom and into a stall so I can turn you visible without freaking everyone out."

We headed towards the bathrooms closest to gate 24 so we don't have to run for the flight. As soon as we entered the stall, we were visible again.

"Flight 823 to Italy, please go to Gate 24 now please." We all ran out of the bathroom and to the gate but there was a problem at the gate.

There were other people at the gate doors waiting to enter the plane. "Guys, I thought this was a private flight?" I quizzed.

"It is supposed to be," Alice said as she approached the desk. "I'm sorry to interrupt and skip the queue but this flight is only supposed to have nine people on it."

The flight attendant looked up at Alice, "Oh Alice, this flight is only for the nine of you," she whispered, "We just have to make it look like its full. These are all undercover flight attendants." Winking at Alice we all understood.

Irish Spy Agency (ISA) Chronicles Book 2: Chain Retrieval

At the back of the queue, Alice explained what was happening so we understood.

As the queue was getting smaller a man and women joined the queue. A flight attendant walked up to them and quietly spoke them, "I'm sorry sir and madam. This flight is fully booked but we can get you next one."

"This is flight 823 to Italy?" he asked. "Yes sir it is." "Here are our tickets we are getting on this flight. No one can stop us."

"I'm sorry sir, but this flight is full. You and your wife will have to wait for the next one," I spoke up, "If you pass on my friend's name Alice Flynn to the airlines you will be fully comped for the next flight to Italy."

"We are getting onto this flight and you can't stop us." He screamed at me. "Sir if you don't stop screaming, you will be removed from the airport," Molly joined in.

"You can't do anything to us," the wife chimed in, "You don't work here."

"No ma'am I don't work here," Molly said taking out her badge, "But I am a Private investigator and can arrest you both. So are these people. Step back and wait for the next flight or you can leave the airport."

The man and his wife were getting very angry at this stage. Alice grabbed myself and the flight attendant as Nick grabbed Molly and pulled us both back. "It's Daniel," Alice screamed.

Irish Spy Agency (ISA) Chronicles Book 2: Chain Retrieval

Still I shock, I was staring at the old man and lady. "Daniel is a young man. This isn't Daniel," I screamed.

As we were looking them, both the man and woman became young. Alice was right.

Daniel and a young woman appeared in front of us. The lady ran for me but Rachel jumped in front of me and kicked her, sending her flying backwards through hole in the wall that Alice had created.

Daniel on the other hand was eyeing me up. "Daniel you're not getting on that plane. I'm not sure what you are up to yet but I will figure it out."

"I want those chains that you stole of me. And I will get the rest," Daniel throw back at me, "and I'll get them before you will."

"Daniel, we already have two of them and no problem with you but we will get the other seven before you as well." Boxing Daniel in, in an invisible box as Alice dealt with the young lady.

"Everyone on the plane now," I screamed. Everyone ran onto the plane except Alice who was keeping the lad in check. "Alice I got this go, get the plane ready to go as soon as I get on," putting the lady into a box like Daniel and running.

Running on to the plane and closing the door. Alice sent us flying down the runway and into the air. Flying through the air as fast as we could.

"We have to get there as fast as possible and get to the Sistine Chapel before Daniel can escape the invisibility box," I said.

Irish Spy Agency (ISA) Chronicles Book 2: Chain Retrieval

"The only way they are getting out of the box is if Daniel creates a portal out of there," Alice said, "But I saw the way you put that box up, if he tries anything it will get smaller. Until you decide it's safe for him to get out."

"I think he has been listening to us somehow about where we are heading," I began, "We are not going home after this. We will continued on the quest on finding these chains.

"We will head to Paul's once we have eight of them to find out where Carabalk Isle is for Molly's chain."

The rest of the flight was very quiet. They was no conversations, even between the flight attendants. The only noise was a small bit of turbulence and the announcements from the pilot.

The flight wasn't that long and when we parachuted out of the plane without parachutes it was great.

I knew Alice used her telekinesis to control our fall to the ground on our bikes for our safety.

"GPS says we have to head this way," Alice said as we drove down the road with Alice in the lead, "I've been here before." She said driving down the road as fast as she could.

As we drove after her, I had to shout at Denny, "This is not a race Denny, so calm down," she looked at me through her helmet and I knew she was annoyed with me. "We have to get there before Daniel not before each other."

Irish Spy Agency (ISA) Chronicles Book 2: Chain Retrieval

We drove around cars the whole way. "How far to go Alice?" I questioned. "The Pantheon is coming up on our right so we have about ten minutes to go but if drive faster it will be quicker."
"Let's drive faster then," I told everyone. We all picked up on our speed. We were driving on one way roads the wrong direction, on roads that no vehicles were allowed.
People were jumping out of the left and right. It was quite hilarious.
"Short cut up here," Alice said as we went up a hill and on to the main road.
"Are we sure?" I questioned her, "It is really a short cut."
"Yes Jackie," she answered, "The museum is up there." I glanced in the direction she pointed and there was the Vatican museums were up ahead.
"They look incredible," I was in shocked, "How are we getting in unnoticed?" "Leave that to Alice and I," Molly said, "We got a plan."
As we arrived at the side of the building. "We got to get in and get out," Alice began, "Jackie, you have to turn everyone invisible and follow myself and Molly in."
"There are more likely to allow two of us in," Molly continued, "Alice got the bikes already sorted. Once we are in you will finally figure out when to turn visible again."

Irish Spy Agency (ISA) Chronicles Book 2: Chain Retrieval

We all nodded and agreed to the plan. Turning everyone but Alice and Molly invisible, we walked inside.

"Polizia Di Stato," Molly and Alice screamed, "Tutti fuori ora." As everyone was running around scared and screaming, but they were leaving the building.

Alice lead the way over to the Sistine Chapel. It was even more beautiful in person than it was in the pictures.

At this point everyone was gone so I turned everyone visible. "Jaden time for phase two of the plan," Molly spoke up, "Can you block the doorway please?"

Looking over at Jaden, I saw him close his eyes and the ground rose up and covered the entrance.

"Now Jackie the places is yours," Alice said, "Time to find the chain."

"Jetpack," I said as I pressed the buttons on my watch. I flew to the ceiling and felt around for an indifference in the painting. But found nothing.

I searched every inch of the ceiling. It took me an hour to do so but still found nothing.

"It's a waste of time," I said as I landed on the floor beside them all and my jetpack disappeared off my back, "There is nothing here." We could hear a commotion outside the barrier so we needed to hurry.

Irish Spy Agency (ISA) Chronicles Book 2: Chain Retrieval

"Jackie, remember what you told us back at Mariana's Trench," Rachel said, "Focus on your power and it will bring you right to the chain."

I closed my eyes and focused. I took a minutes of standing there until I was floating towards the centre of the ceiling.

When I stopped at the ceiling I could see the chain hanging out of the centre of the ceiling. It was exactly like the others but the pendant was an eye that kept fading in and out of view.

As I placed my hand around it, the chain fell into my hand. Instantly I forgot where I was and I fell.

Screaming as I fell I forgot about the team behind me. Only remembering when I stopped an inch away from the floor. Flipping up on to my feet, I had to catch my breath.

"That was close, thanks Alice," I said knowing she caught me. Placing the chain around my neck as I walked towards them.

"Now we need to leave before anyone else gets here," I told them, "Jaden it's time to leave."

Jaden lowered the ground and everyone ran in. people bumped into us and fell down looking confused. No one else could see us.

"Jackie, it's your chain," Rachel said, "It has already connected with you and is working. You've turned us invisible regards of you not trying."

Staring down at my chain I could see the eye go invisible completely.

Irish Spy Agency (ISA) Chronicles Book 2: Chain Retrieval

Running out the door towards the side of the building where we pulled up too. But Daniel and a few goons were waiting for us.

"You are too late Daniel," I shouted at him, "I've already got the chain. I did tell you this, why are you still coming for the chains? And why are you still following us"

"Well I can't have the bad guys winning and getting all the chains, now can I," he answered.

"Alice get into his head and show him we are not the bad guys, the goons he is with are."

Alice did as I asked. She closed her eyes and focus on Daniel. I could see nothing happened for a moment.

All of a sudden Daniel hit the ground. We couldn't see what Alice was doing to him but he was in tears.

Now was our chance to leave. I slowly walked towards my bike and climb on. The gang followed me once they caught on to what I was doing.

We left Daniel in tears on the ground and the goons in agony.

We drove away as fast as we could. "Where to now Jackie?" Denny questioned. "Well I was thinking since we were so close," I answered, "Why not head to Egypt to get Jaden's chain."

"Good idea," Rachel chimed in, "Let's head for the airport." "Let's head towards Roma Ciampino airport and fly over Egypt."

Irish Spy Agency (ISA) Chronicles Book 2: Chain Retrieval

As we continued to drive down the road, I was following Alice and we were taking all these turns and it felt like it was going to take ages to get to the airport. "Alice, time to fly."

She probably knew what I was thinking because she made the bikes fly while I was talking.

"This is going to be so much faster than driving on all those bends," I started, "And we need to get to Egypt before Daniel and the goons do."

The higher we went the more excited I was getting. "Let go," Alice screamed at us. I wasn't paying much attention so wasn't sure what she was talking about.

Seeing everyone let go off their bikes, terrified I dropped mine. We are in the air and our bikes were the only thing keeping us up but then again nothing about the ISA is normal so I was happy to go with it.

Our jetpacks appeared on our backs. "Let's just go straight to Egypt on these makes it easier and Daniel and the goons won't expect it."

"Yes, but it's also a nine hour flight on a plane" Alice spoke, "It will take so much longer on these and we need to get as fast as possible."

"You can speed things up as much as we want though it will be a short flight on these too." I stated.

"Yes, that's true Jackie," Alice said, "But I can't do it that much just yet. My powers are limited until I get my chain."

Irish Spy Agency (ISA) Chronicles Book 2: Chain Retrieval

"My bad Alice," I apologized, "It was only a thought." "No need to apologize." Alice said as we flew towards Roma Ciampino airport.

We followed Alice through the skies as she knew where she was going and we landed on the tarmac of Roma Ciampino airport in no time.

Realising we were not supposed to be here I turned everyone invisible so we wouldn't set off the alarm and let people go crazy.

Walking towards our plane I bumped in the airport staff on the ground because I was so focused on our plane. Alice jumped in before I could say anything and confused the staff member.

Time to pay more attention to my surroundings, I said to myself. "Screw this, let's go," I screamed as I started to run."

Everyone followed suit and we jumped and flipped over people and luggage vans or whatever they are called.

Our plane doors opened as soon as we reached the bottom of the steps. Racing inside to sit down we were all out of breath and sat in silence as the doors closed and we took off.

I was about to tell the team the plan but I was still trying to catch my breath. I downed the glass of water Séan my personal flight attendant had place in front of me.

Catching my breath after drinking the fresh water was so refreshing.

Irish Spy Agency (ISA) Chronicles Book 2: Chain Retrieval

"The plan when we get over the pyramids, we will not all be leaving the plane. Before you all argue with me, Alice said it. We need to get all these chains faster than Daniel and the goons.

"Jaden has to go obviously, Alice will stay here with Denny, Peter, and Molly. Rachel, Mike, Nick and I will go with Jaden.

"We will go down there and get the chain and come straight back here where we will fly to Texas to get Alice and Mike's chains." Everyone nodded in agreement.

Alice closed her eyes at this point to concentrate on getting us to Egypt. While the rest of us dosed off to regain some energy as we go off to save the world.

"We are here," Alice said shaking me awake. As Jaden, Rachel, Mike, Nick and I got up to leave we shook ourselves awake.

"We shall be back as soon as we get the chains," I said as I nodded at Alice. "Strap in everyone else." They all strapped themselves in as Alice opened the door.

The four of us jumped out of the plane. I slowed everyone down with a force field so we would not die. I glanced down as I was lowering us down, "Jaden there is over hundred pyramids in Egypt, we are just at the three in Giza. It's up to you now on which one we go to."

As I looked over at Jaden he was already focus on his power. I took hold of his hand so we could join powers and he could lower us where we needed to go.

As we drew closer to the middle pyramid, "Nick and Rachel you guys stay here and protect us. Whie Mike and I will head in with Jaden." Nick duplicated himself and surrounded the pyramid and Rachal stood beside the real Nick.

We jumped off the force field and landed on the side of the pyramid.

Chapter 8: Rebekah Clark

Jaden closed his eyes as were struggling to keep holding onto the pyramid. As Mike and I focused on Jaden we started to phased through the pyramid. It was so cool as the pyramid enveloped us.
Inside the pyramid was crazy, it was a lot smaller than I thought it was going to be. We needed light.
I'm guessing Jaden already sense that because all of a sudden a light appeared and illuminated the entire pyramid.
They were so many stairs. We were all flying down rather than walking because we needed to

Irish Spy Agency (ISA) Chronicles Book 2: Chain Retrieval

hurry. We saw the king's chambers on the way down.

My knowledge of Egyptian lore was so wrong. I assumed the most important jewels would be left with the king but we were still heading down the stairs.

Jaden brought us both all the way down to the bottom of the pyramid.

As we entered the queen's chamber. Jaden was gone from in front of us and was instantly at the queen's sarcophagus.

Mike and I stood there in shock of what we were seeing. Jaden stood there and it looked like he was speaking to someone but no one else was there.

While we were still staring at him, something appeared in his hand. From where we were we couldn't actually see it but it looked like a chain.

He came over to us and it turned out to be his chain. It looked incredible.

The mountain pendant was amazing. As Jaden placed in on his neck he spoke, "Let's get out of here before anyone else comes."

We all flew up the stairs and Jaden phased us through the pyramid again. Nick and Rachel were still outside waiting on us.

Rachel a about to say something so I stopped her. "Let's get on to the plane before we chat before anyone else shows up."

Irish Spy Agency (ISA) Chronicles Book 2: Chain Retrieval

We flew up towards the plane, I was about to ask Alice to open up but the door was already opened as soon as we reached it.

Alice closed the door as we all entered and sat down.

"So, Jaden who were you talking to back there before you got the chain?" Mike quizzed as the pilot's flew off towards Texas.

"The queen," Jaden began. We must have looked shocked so he continued.

"As soon as I got the queen's sarcophagus, and I was focusing on my power to get the chain, she sat up and looked at me."

We all still so shocked, Alice looked at Jaden and his thoughts were projected in front of us.

Mike and I were look as confused as we did in the background of his thoughts.

We could hear the conversation between Jaden and the queen.

"What is happening?" Jaden asked as confused as the rest of us. "You are here seeking the ISA earth chain, yes?"

"Of course I am." "Many has come before you seeking it and failed. What makes you any different?"

"I need the chain to make the world safer, rogue agents are destroying the planet with other rogue agents. This chain will help us stop them and protect the planet and everyone in it."

Irish Spy Agency (ISA) Chronicles Book 2: Chain Retrieval

The queen placed one hand on Jaden's chest and the other on his head and closed her eyes.

"I see you intention is to use it for good and protect the planet. You may have it as long as that is your intent. If that changes it will automatically come back to me."

She handed Jaden the chain and fell backwards in the sarcophagus. Jaden then snapped out of whatever trance he was in and came to stand before Mike and I.

The memory faded and we are still in shocked until the pilot broke us out. "Ladies and Gentleman, we have unfortunately hit a turbulence storm as we fly to Texas." Alice stood up then and head towards the cockpit.

"I'm guessing she's gone to help get past the turbulence because she can't fly a plane too. Or can she?" I quizzed Nick. "She can fly a plane but this time she going to help with the turbulence," he replied.

We all strapped in to get ready for a bumpy ride. What happened next surprised us all. Alice came running out of the cockpit.

"We have to make a quick and safe landing," Alice screamed at us, "The pilots are dead, that was one of Daniel's goons speaking. The plane is falling."

Nick followed Alice backed into the cockpit. The rest of us tried not to panic when an idea popped into my head.

Irish Spy Agency (ISA) Chronicles Book 2: Chain Retrieval

"Séan, an féidir leat na freastalaithe eitlte go léir a thabhairt le chéile, le do thoil?" (Can you get all the flight attendants together, please?) As Séan gathered all the flight attendants and staff, I filled the team in on my plan. "I'm going to open a portal to send them all to Paul where it is safe and let him know what is happening here."
Séan gathered everyone and I told him, "Tá mé á chur chuig Pól agat. (I'm sending you to Paul's.) Líon isteach é ar a bhfuil ag tarlú. (Fill him in on everything.) Abair leis go bhfuil muid slán sábháilte agus mbeidh muidar ais go luath, (Tell him we are safe and will be back soon,)" as I opened the portal.
Séan gave me a quick hug and a nod before he followed everyone else through the portal.
"At least those guys are all safe," I said looking at everyone else. "Now we must protect each other."
I was looking at each of my new friends and was trying to figure out how I was going to protect each of them. Alice and Nick both ran out of the cockpit together.
"We got to jump now," the both scream at us. She threw opened the door fast and we were all sucked out the door. Everything happened so fast, none of us were ready.
Instinctively, my power drew everyone together into an invisible force field. "What happened, Alice?" I questioned just as the plane above us blew up.

Irish Spy Agency (ISA) Chronicles Book 2: Chain Retrieval

"The goons sent a bomb our direction and I tried my best to blow it up before it got to us but nothing was working. We had to jump before we died,"

Alice was looking around us as she answered me. "Jackie can you land us on that land over there. I know exactly where we are and we can get help."

I followed Alice's direction and landed on the huge piece of land. When we touch the ground the force field disappeared and I noticed we were on a ranch somewhere in the America.

"Alice, where are we?" A few of us asked at the same time, so confused on what was happening.

Before she answered though a woman came out of the house screaming and pointing a gun at us, "You have to the count of three to get the hell off my property before I shoot."

This woman looked so familiar, her shoulder length red hair and extremely strong country accent. I just couldn't figure it out where I knew her from.

"Rebekah, you don't have to shoot," Alice spoke up, "My name is Alice Flynn and I am an agent with Irish Spy Agency. We need your help." Alice showed Rebekah her ID badge and Rebekah just nodded.

"That wasn't y'all up there was it," Rebekah asked pointing to the plane still falling from the sky. "Unfortunately, Rebekah it was us. The enemy we are up against right now just tried to kill us," Alice answered, "For now they believe they have killed us. Can we rest before we continue on with our mission?"

"Follow me," Rebekah said as she walked into her house. I was still confused on what was happening but because Alice and Nick followed her, so did I and the team followed me.

Rebekah's house is absolutely beautiful. Wooden frames everywhere, sliding doors as entrances into rooms. "We are sorry for intruding…"Alice began but Rebekah cut her off.

"My family have always been prepared for when the ISA needed our help. My parents trained me and their parents before them and so on. I have trained my kids as well."

"Rebekah Clark?" I asked in shocked as my team looked at me, "Sorry, I've been trying to figure out how I knew you. Are you Rebekah Clark one of the many queens of country music?"

"Is that what people are calling me?" Rebekah answered. "My parents and I love your music," I screamed

"I'm honoured to meet a fan," Rebekah said, "Would you like a picture?" Jumping at the chance to have a picture with Rebekah I just nodded.

Alice took my phone off me and I stood beside Rebekah. Taking a couple of photos of the two off us. When we finished she told us to sit down around the table.

Irish Spy Agency (ISA) Chronicles Book 2: Chain Retrieval

"This is the biggest team from the ISA my family has ever seen," Rebekah said, "How come this team is so big?"

"Well Peter, Molly, Denny, Jaden, Mike, and Rachel were a team," Alice stated, "They grew up together but joined the agency at different times. But Paul O'Rourke joined the six as a team.

"Myself and my husband Nick here were hired at their school as Special Needs Assistants to watch over them without them knowing obviously."

"I was walking through the corridor one day and overheard the six of them talking about a mission," I inserted, "I was confused because I was wondering if they were talking about a spy mission or just a mission to get someone a present.

"After school, I followed them right into their lair with Paul. He gave them a mission and gave me the power of invisibility."

"This isn't Jackie's fault but at this stage everything went downhill," Rachel chimed in, "We were introduced to Daniel who has every power and more powers are growing."

"Daniel was becoming our new teacher and the enemy we are fighting now wanted him but kidnapped Peter here instead," Denny said.

"They had me under some sort of mind control," Peter announced, "This made me see my friends as enemies. I left Molly here for dead at one point."

"This went on for ages," Molly interjected, "Jackie came up with a plan and we got Peter back.

Irish Spy Agency (ISA) Chronicles Book 2: Chain Retrieval

And we were joined by Alice and Nick as team members."

"There was a big fight in our school about two weeks ago and Daniel lost his memories completely," Mike said, "He has blamed us for it all."

"With Daniel working with the bad guys," Jaden announced, "Paul sent us on a mission to collect nine chains that were lost to the ISA years and years ago.

"We have found four so far and we were on the way to Abilene Texas to get the fourth and fifth one when the goons working with Daniel bombed us out of the sky."

"We need the chains to stop Daniel and the goons," Nick said, "Because if Daniel gets them all the world is doomed."

"Well," Rebekah spoke up, "A lot has happened over the past couple of months. Jackie welcome to the ISA. Well you can rest here for as long as you want until you need to continue your mission."

"Thank you, Rebekah," I said, "I'm going to step outside for a moment. Need a bit of fresh air."

Everyone nodded at me as I rose form the table walked towards the door we entered in. As I reached for the door metal came down and covered it.

All this happened to the windows as well. "Guys, what is happening?" I questioned.

Irish Spy Agency (ISA) Chronicles Book 2: Chain Retrieval

"The house is under attack," Rebekah stated, "The house protects itself from any harm. Y'all can leave this way."

Rebekah lead us all the way over to the back wall. "This leads to a tunnel about a mile down so you will need to jump." She pressed a button on the wall. And the floor opened.

"Go now, and may y'all be safe," Rachel and Denny jumped first, followed by Jaden and Mike. Alice and Nick were about to jump but I grabbed her arm.

"We can't just leave," I said, "We have to stay and fight. I guarantee that it's Daniel and the goons. They have figured out we survived that explosion."

Looking down the hole , I screamed down at the guys, "Hold on," using my powers I dragged them all back up to us.

"Rebekah, I know you want us safe but we have these powers and the people out there also have powers. Once we get rid of them, we will leave."

Rebekah was about to argue when I stopped her, "I know you want us to leave because you can protect yourself but we have a better chance of surviving than you do."

She stepped back and nodded. "Go to the safe room and lock yourself in. I'll come find you when we are finished," Alice stated. Rebekah ran away from us.

Irish Spy Agency (ISA) Chronicles Book 2: Chain Retrieval

"Alice lift the metal doors surrounding us, " I commanded, "We will take this fight outside." We all went into fight mode. Alice opened the metal doors.

"Follow me," I said walking out the door. The scene in front of us would have sent people hiding. Daniel and the goons had surrounded us. There was about fifteen feet between the door and Daniel.

Alice stood beside me on the right, while Nick, Rachel and Jaden stood beside her. Peter stood to my left with Molly, Mike and Denny.

"Daniel, why did you come here? I shouted at him, "You and the goons always lose against us yet you always come back for more."

"You forget, we want the chains that around your neck. When we get them, we will kill you all and get the rest," he screamed back.

"That will never happen," We all shouted back at him. We got ready to fight when Rebekah burst through the door with one of those round machine guns that helicopters have, with what seem liked a never ending ream of bullets.

"Get the hell off my property," She screamed, "Or you will regret it." Daniel or the goons never looked more like laughing than they did now.

"Rebekah, you are going to get hurt," I screamed back, "If you don't leave now." She shook her head at me. "I'm not leaving, I told you i have been prepare all of this. These goons better leave."

Daniel and the goons laughed at her before they attacked. As they ran towards us the all fell to the ground in pain.

"Alice, what are you doing?" I quizzed. "It's not me Jackie," she answered, "Even if it was me, I wouldn't be able to do it to them all."

As we all looked around confused, Rebekah was smirking, "I did warn them," she said laughing. Looking back at her we couldn't help it but joined in with her laughter.

"What's happening?" I asked in between laughter. "I did tell you my family were trained to protect ourselves by the ISA, they also helped protect the house and the ground.

"If you come with the intent of harming anyone in the house or on the ground, you will be in intense pain like they are all right now. You guys can do what you want with them now. They're not going anywhere."

We were all still laughing at what was going on before I looked at everyone, "We can all open portal and send them off somewhere."

"Where do we send them all?" Denny asked. "Let's send to Nullarbor, to the Bunda Cliffs. Where we found the map. That's the furthest away from here."

They all nodded at me and we pressed the buttons on our watches and said, "To Nullarbor, to the Bunda Cliffs."

Irish Spy Agency (ISA) Chronicles Book 2: Chain Retrieval

One giant portal open in front of us and as I looked at Alice, she already knew what I was thinking and she pushed the portal towards Daniel and the goons.

Every single one of them disappeared. "That will show them to mess with the ISA," Rebekah said and we all laughed again.

"Thank you for your help Rebekah," I said when we stopped laughing, "We would love to take you up on your offer to stay but I think it is best for everyone that we head on to Abilene now and save the world."

"That can wait until tomorrow Jackie," Rebekah answered me, "It's getting too dark to travel anywhere now. You can travel tomorrow after a refreshing night sleep and a shower."

Knowing none of us would win this, we followed Rebekah back inside.

She brought us back to the same wall where she opened the door in the ground but pressed the other button and a male robot voice asked, "How many?"

"Four men and five ladies," Rebekah answered. Two doors appeared on the wall. Men on the right and ladies on the left.

"There is enough beds and showers for each of you. There is also a change of clothes for each of you and pj's." Rebekah told us as she opened the doors.

Irish Spy Agency (ISA) Chronicles Book 2: Chain Retrieval

"Thank you so much for everything Rebekah," I spoke up, "My parents are going to be so jealous when we get home."

"Slumber party," Denny yelled as she ran into the room, followed by Rachel and Molly. "Breakfast will be ready at 8am."

"Thanks again Rebekah," Alice and I both said as we walked into the room to the girls. Denny and Molly were ready for a shower while Rachel was getting ready.

As I got ready for the shower, it finally dawned on me how wrecked I was. Jumping in the shower, I raced through my shower so I could go to sleep.

Denny was already lying in her bed when I got back into my bed.

"I hope you're ready for some girl-talk Jackie," Denny squealed, "Some beans are going to be spilt tonight."

"Unfortunately not Denny," I answered, "I'm wrecked tired. My body is ready to crash. Remember I'm new this life."

"It's O.K. Jackie," Molly said from behind me, "Denny is the only one ready for an all-nighter. My energy is so depleted right now."

"So is mine," Alice stated heading to her bed.
"Same here," Rachel announced jumping into her bed.

Within minutes of getting into bed, all the ladies were asleep and as much as I tried to sleep, my mind wouldn't shut off.

Irish Spy Agency (ISA) Chronicles Book 2: Chain Retrieval

Staring at the ceiling, trying to dose of but sleep just did not want to come to me.

With my mind racing, thinking about how much this team has been through since I joined the team. Hours went by and still no sleep.

I spent my time thinking about what we are going to do when we got all nine chains. How we were going to get Daniel back, even though I have a few ideas on how that's going to happen.

I'm also worried about how everyone is going to react to who is the boss of the goons, especially Paul and Daniel, when we get him back.

Time went by really fast because before I knew it was nearly 8am so I went for another quick shower to wash the lack of sleep off me.

During the shower I could hear someone in the kitchen, so I slowly got out of the shower, dried myself as fast as I could so I could get dress and see who is in the kitchen.

I threw on a tracksuit and a hoodie, something easy in case I needed to fight.

Slowly creeping to the kitchen, making sure none of the doors creak or made any noise. As soon as I got there I just needed to say, "Good Morning Rebekah." She was making breakfast for everyone.

"Oh Jackie," Rebekah said, "Good Morning, how are you doing? Sleep well." She must have noticed a look on my face before she looked at the clock.

Irish Spy Agency (ISA) Chronicles Book 2: Chain Retrieval

"Never mind," Rebekah chuckled. "You need any help?" I asked, "My father is a chef so I know how to cook everything."

She laughed again. "Of course not, you are a guess here," she said, "You will sit and have a coffee, or tea, or juice. I will do all the cooking."

To avoid the argument, I sat at the table and poured an apple juice for myself. "It was a long night," I stated, "I wanted to sleep but it avoid me."

"What did you instead?" she asked me. "I was trying to figure out some plans," I answered, "There is somethings the team needs to know but I can't say anything yet because no-one will want to continue on the mission and we need to get Daniel back before I tell them."

"My mind races too when I need to write new music," She assured me, "It does get easier. It's not easy being in charge is it?"

"No," I admitted, "I'm new to this life and new to having friends and they wanted me in charge. I don't think I'll sleep for a while." I continued laughing.

"Everything will get easier especially when you have people who can help alongside you." She would have continued but everyone had joined us.

Everone joined us at the table to eat breakfast. Sitting in silence as we enjoyed a homecooked meal.

Rachel and Denny finished first so they started washing dishes as we all packed up all the dishes.

Irish Spy Agency (ISA) Chronicles Book 2: Chain Retrieval

"There is a dishwasher here ladies," Rebekah said as she showed them. While the rest of us tidied everything up before we left.

"Rebekah, thank you for everything," I announced when we were ready, "Can you tell us the fastest way to get to Abilene Texas?"

"Yes, of course I can," Rebekah said walking away from us, "You could drive there on the road or you can use my tunnel that is connected to my brother's house in there. I'll ring him when you are gone to let him know y'all are on the way."

With each of us giving Rebekah a hug goodbye and another thanks we all jumped down the hole.

Our bikes were already waiting on us down there. Putting our helmets on and hopping onto our bikes, we headed off down the tunnel.

Chapter 9: Jacob's Ladder, Texas

There was so many turns and bends in these tunnel but the good thing was we did not need to slow down at all. We drove at top speed so we could finished this mission soon.

I drove on a head of everyone else so I could see what was ahead. When I got to the end of the tunnel. With an invisible force field under me I raised myself up to the top.

Knocking on the door, but getting ready to fight if I needed too. I didn't want to put my team in any danger.

Ready to fight as the door opened, I was waiting for a few minutes before I heard my team below me so I sent another force field down to stop them coming up.

The door slowly opened above me, "Jackie it's ok," a man said, " Rebekah is my sister she told me you were coming."

I jumped up in front of him. "How did you know it was me?" "Rebekah picked up on your strong will to protect your team so I figured you would be the first up."

As I focus on this man who still had not told me his name I let my team come up without letting him know. Something was off here, I could feel it.

I knew Alice would be ready to fight because she could hear me screaming in my head. "What else did Rebekah say?" I asked giving him a chance to introduce himself.

"Just that you were an incredible team who would do anything for each other," he answered.

He walked away from me at this point so I said to Alice, "Let everyone know I've turned you invisible, something's not right up here."

I followed the man as I sense my team was getting closer to me. "So how long you lived here?" I quizzed him, still waiting on a name.

"Well this is the family home," he answered, "I inherited it." Now I know this isn't Rebekah's brother. Rebekah got the family home. I know this because my parents and I have followed her career forever.

"Who are you?" I questioned, "And what have you done to Rebekah's brother?"

My team had arrived at this time. Alice threw him into a wall and force him there, "It's Daniel," she said as she force him back into Daniel.

"Daniel got here about thirty minutes ago after he heard Rebekah talk to her brother," Alice explained.

As I looked at Daniel, I lifted my hands up and push them together. I closed Daniel into a small box that he won't get out of. The box was about knee high.

"Jackie, where did you learn to do that?" Rachel asked me. "I have no idea," I laughed, "I just did it." We all laughed.

"Time to send him somewhere in the world," Alice said. "Send him back to Italy," I said laughing, "We'll deal with as soon as this mission is over."

As I said Italy a portal opened and went towards Daniel. "Try get out of this box," I laughed as he disappeared.

"Nick, can you leave a few duplicates here to look for Rebekah's brother as we head to Abilene Christian University?" Nick nodded as three more Nicks appeared behind us.

We all walked outside to where our bikes were waiting on us. But as soon as we approached they became two SUV's vehicles.

"Ladies in one and the men in the other," Alice spoke up, "These are safer on the roads here."

Irish Spy Agency (ISA) Chronicles Book 2: Chain Retrieval

As we approached the vehicles, Alice threw keys at me, "You are driving." I was so excited I ran to the right side of the vehicle. Everyone laughed at me.

"Jackie, Americans drive on the other side of the road here so they vehicles are the opposite way around too," Denny told me.

Walking around the driver side of the vehicle and getting in. I was going to have to really concentrate driving here.

Everyone climbed in, Alice beside me and Denny in the middle of the back seat. Molly was on the right and Rachel on the left.

As I drove off I realised I had no idea where I was going. "Alice, how do I get there?" "I was waiting for you to ask," She said.

Not answering my question but he pointed at the radio. She press a few buttons and an automatic voice spoke up, "Turn right in 500 feet."

The only sound in the SUV as I drove was the sat-nav telling me where to go. The ladies were all a sleep as I drove down the highway.

It took about sixteen minutes to get Abilene Christian University. It was huge.

As I reverse into the car space, I woke the ladies up. Jumping out of the SUV and looking around the place, I would love to come to place like this when I finished school.

We all surround the monument trying to figure out what to do. We got Nick to take pictures of us all from different points at the monument. At one point it was amazing.

A cross was formed with the way the rocks were placed and as I looked around there was so many rocks with different words on them:

"Whoever enters through the gate."

"Well of Water."

This place is beginning to become my favourite place in the entire world. "So guys, we are all not going to help Alice and Mike get their chains because we need to split up," I announced.

"So who is going with Alice and Mike?" Denny asked. "Well Nick, Rachel, Peter and I will stay here and protect the students and the monument. Molly, Denny and Jaden will go with them."

Denny cheer so loud that people started to look at us. "Denny, keep it down," I shouted.

"Alice let everyone know the following plan: You are going to make it look like we are still here while I turned Molly, Denny, Jaden and you and Mike invisible so you can go get the chains. The rest of us shall be here waiting for you all."

I turned them all invisible and said, "Now focus on your powers and go get those chains.

As Alice and Mike closed their eyes something really rare happened. The moon was on top of the ladder. They all climb the ladder beside the representation of the angels from Jacob's dream in the Bible.

Right as they jumped onto the moon they were gone and so was the moon.

The rest of us stayed where we were so we could be here if anything happened.

We waited on the grass as it was too warm to do anything. It was about forty-five degrees celsius. We did have a water fight to cool down but of course Rachel won.

As we focus on the water fight we never noticed the students and the teachers came and were watching us. Looking at them, we nodded at them and they joined in.

Everyone was laughing and throwing water balloons at each other. This was happening for a long time until a few of the students noticed that Rachel had no balloons but was still throwing water at people.

"How can you do that?" a few of the students ask at the same time, "How are able to control water like that. "It's all in your head," Rachel said but they didn't believe her.

"Nah, there is something else going on here, one of them said, "I will figure it out." Going back to the water fight it was great until some of them figured it out.

"Y'all are from Ireland," one of the students screamed, "You were all part of that that small town being destroyed. The teenagers with superpowers."

We were all silent while everyone slowly stopped throwing the water balloons and stare at us. Not answering anyone's questions, we were frozen as they threw accusations at us.

"You shouldn't have done any of that." "Get out of here before you destroy our school." "Use your powers and leave."

Just as I was about to open my mouth, the moon reappeared at the top of the ladder and the gang jumped to the ground.

Everyone went quiet at seeing this. The shouting began again as it all sunk in. Some on our side and some against us.

It got that rowdy as they surrounded us, Alice had to push everyone back away from us. "We have to leave now," I screamed, "Keep them back as we all get to the SUV's."

We all ran back to the SUV's as Alice kept everyone off us. When we were all in, opening the windows and screaming at the boys, "Get out of here now." The boys drove off away as Alice ran to us and jumped into the vehicle.

Speeding down the road, "We have to get off the road now," Alice said, "Some of them have decided to follow us."

We couldn't see how far the boys were. "Alice, tell the boys to stay where they are until we catch up," I told her as I drove in and around cars, "I'm

Irish Spy Agency (ISA) Chronicles Book 2: Chain Retrieval

going to turn everyone invisible and you are going to make sure they see us go the wrong way."

We drove towards the airport in Abilene to fly home so we can get Nick's chain then Peter's and finally Molly's chain.

It took us 12 minutes to get to Abilene Regional Airport. We drove into the carpark and park our cars. It will be easier to fly for forty minutes than drive for three hours to Dallas.

Heading into the airport and straight to the counter to check in. Alice and Nick went up to the counter to buy our tickets given that the are they only adults here.

"Can we buy flights here to Shannon Airport, Ireland? Kinda a last minute travel," Alice said to the lady behind the counter. "Of course you can, we just need to see some I.D." The lady announced.

Alice and Nick both took out their I.D. and showed the lady, "Here you go." They lady glanced at them, "Perfect, how many seats are we booking today?

"There is nine of us altogether," Nick responded. "Perfect the total is $3,658.86," the lady replied. "Are you sure?" Nick asked reshowing the lady his I.D.

The Lady looked up from the counter and double checked Nick's ID. "Oh sorry sir," She replied, "Let me add your badge number to the ticket's."

Irish Spy Agency (ISA) Chronicles Book 2: Chain Retrieval

As she typed in the badge number, "Your new price is free. Can I get names for the tickets please."

"Here you go," Alice said as she handed a piece of paper to the lady. After a couple of minutes the lady handed Nick the nine tickets. "Thank you. Enjoy your day."

Nick handed us all tickets just as we stood in the security line. "Please take off belts, watches or anything metal and place them in the buckets and walk through the machines," The security team all said.

I lead my team through security and as soon as they saw us, they were about to repeat it to me until Alice said to me in my head, *"Show them your badge."*

Taking my badge out to show them, they pressed a button on the side of the machine and told me to step through.

I was thinking the machine was going to beep because I still had my watch on but it was silent. The ISA think of everything I thought laughing to myself.

The plane was already boarding as we approached so we went straight on. As we sat down the flight attendants went through all the safety measures.

They knew we were all going to be safe if anything happen to everyone here. Every seat was full on this flight.

Irish Spy Agency (ISA) Chronicles Book 2: Chain Retrieval

We chatted about absolutely nothing just to pass the time. It was a thirty minute flight so we were in Dallas in no time.

Walking through the gate after saying thanks and goodbye to the flight attendants, there were other flight attendants with our Alice and Nicks names on a sign.

As we approached them Alice and Nick showed them their I.D. and we were on our way. I was so excited to fly home.

Feels like it's been weeks since I saw my parents or Paul but it's been less than a week. But I knew we could not see them until we got all the chains.

As we flew back to Ireland, we all slept except a clone of Nick who kept watch to make sure nothing was going to happen this time.

Nick's clone woke us up as the plane landing in Shannon airport. The plane pulled right up to the gate as we stood and stretched.

We walked straight through security without any hassle. "Where to now?" I asked, "I've no idea where we are."

Everyone looked around as confused as I was. "Alice and I know where we are going," Nick said heading outside. We followed them out the door and were heading to the carpark when Molly shouted at us, "Guys our bikes are over there."

We turned around to look where Molly was looking and our bikes were really there.

Irish Spy Agency (ISA) Chronicles Book 2: Chain Retrieval

"Guys we need to hurry back to Paul," I began as we walk towards the bikes, "So I think we should bring the bikes through the portals."

"We'll take the bikes into the carpark with us and go from there," Alice announced.

They all jumped onto their bikes, "Jackie, get on your bike and follow us," Nick said. Jumping on to my bike I followed them through the carpark.

Driving through all the carparks trying to find an empty one so we could open a portal. We drove all over the carparks trying to find an empty place.

We eventually had to leave the airport to find somewhere safe. Driving around for fifteen minutes we couldn't find anywhere.

"Let's just drive the whole way there," I said, "Drive to Galway get the chain and portal to Hookhead." We headed towards the motorway.

Driving way over the speed limit, it was time to finish this mission now. Sooner rather than later.

I've never been away from home for so long without seeing my parents. I really need to see them and fill them in on things before the see us all over the news.

As we drove on the motorway , we kept together but we weaved in and about around cars. It did take us just over an hour to get into Galway city.

The city itself finding was beautiful and as much fun as it would be to explore we need to get onto finding Nick's chain.

Irish Spy Agency (ISA) Chronicles Book 2: Chain Retrieval

"Nick we are here in the city now," I said as we all pulled over to the side of the road, "You need to lead us the rest of the way."

Nick and I drove side by side as the rest followed us in twos. I was following slightly behind Nick as he drove in and out of traffic as well as left and right turns.

If felt like it was hours of driving before Nick pulled into a huge field.

Chapter 10: Hippodrome Aeon Circus, Galway & Hookhead Lighthouse, Wexford

This circus was huge. From the outside it looked like it everything from trapeze artists to clowns. We could hear animals inside but they were no stables around outside.

That does only mean one thing: there are not using real animals. Whoever thought about not using real animals was a genius.

"Some German circus was the first to do it, Jackie," Alice said as we walked towards the entrance.

"Nine tickets is nine euro," said the lady in the ticket box at the entrance. So cheap I thought,

they must be making their money to be able to charge so little.
Alice paid and after giving us a wristband each we entered. Walking around we could see so much. Separate tents for all different shows and acts or whatever they do here.
They had clowns making balloons. People doing sword tricks and people setting pois on fire and doing some tricks.
We got closer to the centre and I was about to talk to Nick when I could hear people move but couldn't see them. Not knowing what was about to happen I needed to protect all the chains.
Turning them all invisible and making sure that Daniel couldn't get them. That was the last thing I remembered when everything went black.

*   *   *

I had no idea how long we were all out but as I woke up I could hear a couple of voices arguing. I couldn't hear exactly what they talking about. Slowly moving my head around to see where my team was.
We were all tied up and gagged. I was very confused about what was happening. *"Alice."* I called out in my head but I heard nothing back. I

Irish Spy Agency (ISA) Chronicles Book 2: Chain Retrieval

looked around trying to find Alice but she wasn't here.

I stood up and shook the gag off me. "What the heck is going on here?" The two women looked at me.

"Where are the chains?" one of them screamed at me. "Wouldn't you like to know," I laughed. They looked really annoyed with me which made laugh even more.

"You better tell me," she screamed at me, "Or your friends here will get it." "Now if I tell you, then I can't have some fun."

"What do you mean by that?" She looked confused. "Well there is this," I said as I kicked her in the mouth sending her flying backwards.

As this encounter was happening, I was slowly unravelling the rope around my wrist.

The other woman jump in front of me to attack but she failed as I kicked her across the room as well. I jumped down off the trailer where we were all sitting on.

It was now two on one as the two women started to fight me. I was so happy my training at the ISA Camp Duo was coming in handy.

Blocking and hitting them was so much fun but I knew this had to end so I sent them flying into the wall behind us knocking them out.

I raced back over to my team that was here. When I reached them I noticed it was only Molly, Peter, and Nick were the only ones here.

Irish Spy Agency (ISA) Chronicles Book 2: Chain Retrieval

As I was shaking them awake, they were confused on what was happening. "Don't worry," I said, "We'll figure it out as a team."
I untied Nick and then he duplicated himself to untie Molly and Peter. "Nick you take Peter and go find your chain," I announced, "Molly and I will go find the others."
They all nodded at me. Nick closed his eyes, "This way Peter." And they both left.
"Are you happy to split up Molly or do we search together?" I questioned. "Best sticking together. In case anything else happens."
We slowly made our way out of the tent we were in. Turning myself and Molly invisible as we walked outside.
We were slowly jumping over stuff and still hiding though we were invisible. Daniel was here at one point. He is the only one able to take us out. We were not sure if he was still here or not.
As we made our way around the filed slowly, something caught my eye. Poking Molly, "Can you see that clearly?" I asked pointing the what I saw.
She shook head so we both moved closer. What we saw shock us both. Whoever is running this circus is making Alice, Denny, Rachel, Mike, and Jaden perform in the main event tonight.
"We have to get them out of here before this happens," Molly said so worried. "Oh we will Molly," I promised, "We'll get them back. Let's head this way."

Irish Spy Agency (ISA) Chronicles Book 2: Chain Retrieval

"Alice, can you hear me?" "Jackie, where are you?" "We are looking for you guys. Where are you?" "We are all in cages in the main tent. We can't out. I can't get out." "Alice we are coming to get you all. We'll be there soon."

"Molly," I said pointing, "The team is over there in the main tent." Slowly making our way to the main tent to rescue our team. We really needed to get them and get the heck out of here.

We slowly crept into the tent and headed towards the back . We approached the team quietly when we found them. I reached up to release the rope tied around them but was hit in the head from behind again.

*   *   *

I definitely had no idea how long I was knocked out this time but I knew it was a long time because it was dark outside.

Molly was the only one still with me. The others were gone again. "Where is everyone Molly?" I quizzed. "They were taken just a few minutes ago," Molly told me, "They are being forced to use their powers for entertainment."

"Molly we will get them back," I said, " I keep my promises. "How though, we are all tied up?" she quizzed me while she cried. "Because Molly," I began, as Peter and Nick jumped up on the trailer

Irish Spy Agency (ISA) Chronicles Book 2: Chain Retrieval

Molly and I were on, "This time we are not on our own." Nick and Peter untied us so we could stand up.

"You got the chain Nick?" Molly asked as we went running after our team. We both saw him nodded as we went running into the main tent.

On entering the tent, Daniel was in there torturing Alice in the corner while Denny, Mike, Rachel, and Jaden were performing in the middle of the tent for the audience.

The were all cheering and laughing. Daniel was electrocuting Alice in a pool but he kept her from dying. "I'm going to get Alice, you guys get the others," I screamed at the other guys.

I knew Nick would be too emotional to rescue Alice.

Alice saw me coming so she distracted Daniel for me. "So Daniel, why did you take me to try and kill me? Why not Peter or Molly or Denny or any other or the guys?"

"Well if you must know, it's about Jackie," he began, "Jackie has the power of invisibility and without her we can't get all the chains."

I was behind him at this point, "If you want me," I said, "Turn around." As Daniel turned around he faced dropped. I hit him a box in the face and sent him flying through the tent. The tent rip went right up to the top.

As the tent fell apart, I grabbed Alice and we went running towards the others. We reached the

Irish Spy Agency (ISA) Chronicles Book 2: Chain Retrieval

others just as Nick and Peter untied the metal around their neck. "Let's get out of here now," I screamed as we ran outside.

I touched my watch and said, "Hookhead Lighthouse." As the portal opened, we ran straight through. Some people followed through but were sliced in half.

Hookhead is beautiful. I will come back someday with my parents for the tour. "Peter," I looked around until I found him, "Your turn to focus on your powers."

Everyone was focus on the scenery so had I call on them to focus. "Peter we are all going to follow you before we head back to Paul."

Peter closed his eyes and started walking towards the lighthouse. As we got closer to the lighthouse, he turned towards the edge of the cliffs.

We followed silently as he ran up to the edge of the cliff and jump in the ocean. Before he hit the water, he was covered in scuba gear. Following suit, we hit the water in scuba gear as well.

Peter was heading for some underwater cave. I was so confused because Peter's power was Super strength not water.

We all swam after him and he stop at a wall. "Peter, what's happening?" Molly asked him a bit worried.

"My chain lies behind this wall," he began, "But the issue with that is this wall is the cornerstone if

Irish Spy Agency (ISA) Chronicles Book 2: Chain Retrieval

you will. If I break this wall the lighthouse will end up in the sea with everyone up there."

We were all silent in shock, not sure what to do.

"Alice is going to help now that she has her chain," I blurted out, "Peter, break the wall while Alice holds everything else up. Nick and Molly you go help Alice."

"I can't hold up that much weight," Alice stated, "I'm not strong enough." "Alice you are the strongest person I know, and now you have a little help from something little around your neck."

Alice smiled as Molly, Nick and herself left.

"Alice let us know when you are ready so Peter can start."

I could see Peter was ready to break this wall down and get his chain. Within seconds Alice got back to us. "I'm ready," She said. Peter punched the wall as soon as she said the words.

He punched and he punched and was getting very frustrated because nothing was happening.

"Peter," I shouted at him, "Breath and focus." He closed his eyes and slowed his breathing as he swung one more box. The wall shatter and there was his chain.

Peter's chain was like the rest but he had a man lifting weights on his. "Alice, I need you focus now and place the wall back together so nothing bad happens."

Swimming away I took one last look back at the wall as it slid into place like nothing had happened.

Irish Spy Agency (ISA) Chronicles Book 2: Chain Retrieval

We all got together beside the lighthouse as we prepared to head back to Paul's when I could hear my name being called. It was Daniel. He was taunting me into a fight. We do not have the time right now to listen to him. As I was opening up a portal, he pulled all my friends towards him. Racing after them, he had them all tied up. "Don't worry Jackie," He said, "Fight me and I will spare them." My friends all started shouting at me. "We are not worth it Jackie." "Do not give him what he wants." "Save yourself."

I couldn't believe my ears. They were telling to leave them for Daniel to kill them to save myself. I was not that kind of leader who protected themselves over their team.

"I've not got the time, Daniel," I said, "But to save my team, let's fight. No powers or weapons. Hand to hand combat only."

As we stood across from each other in our fighting stance I said, "Daniel, I just want you know before any else tells you. I defeat your records at the ISA official training."

I smirked at him and it seem to rile him up so much. "Let's do this," we both screamed and ran at each other.

Daniel threw the first punch as I slid under his arm and hit him with an uppercut to the right-side of his ribs. It winded him so badly, he collapsed.

Irish Spy Agency (ISA) Chronicles Book 2: Chain Retrieval

"Never start a fight, you are not a hundred percent sure you will win." I broke my own rules of this fight and placed Daniel inside and invisible box and sent him threw a portal somewhere.

I ran over to my team as the binds on them disappeared. "Let's get out of here before anything else happens." I said opening a portal to Paul's lair.

*   *   *

Paul was over the moon too see us as were we. As I mentioned before, it felt like months since we saw each other last.

"We got them all now Paul," Denny said grinning, "Well except Molly's but we are hoping you can tell us where that is now so we can have the collection."

"Breathe Denny," Paul began, " I am just running the finally scan for it now. I found an old book with codes on it from our founders about how to get to Carabalk Isle."

As went into a tale of all our adventures. It took hours telling Paul what we went through on this quest to find the chains and everything Daniel has done.

"I do have a plan to get Daniel back as soon we get Molly's chain," I stated. Everyone became very intrigued in what I was about to say.

Irish Spy Agency (ISA) Chronicles Book 2: Chain Retrieval

"I've been doing a lot thinking," I began, "Everything that we have achieved since we began our search.

"Everything that has worked for us so far has come down to the core four elements we have. Fire, Water, Earth and Air.

"The plan is, Denny, Rachel, Jaden and Mike will channel their power and focus it on Daniel."

"Daniel can be very slippery Jackie," Denny stated, "How can we stop him leaving?"

"I have that in the plan too Denny," I said as everyone burst out laughing, "Alice is going to force Daniel to stay in the one spot so you can hit him with your power.

"The rest of us will help Molly search for her chain because I know Daniel will be there like he has been there for the other chains."

Everyone nodded in agreement. "So everyone needs to head home," Paul said, "Rest up because it's going to be rough couple of days."

" Goodnight Paul," We all said as we left and flew home.

We all landed in our in back yards after saying goodnight to each other. My parents were sitting at the table eating dinner when I entered.

They were excited to see me home. I filled them in on everything. And show them some pictures that I had taken of the different places we had been. They were just as amazed as I was.

Irish Spy Agency (ISA) Chronicles Book 2: Chain Retrieval

"Some of these places we will have visited. Let me get some time off from the agency some time." They were both very excited with that news. "as much as I would to stay up and chat. It's been a long few weeks and we got more to go."

Kissing both parents on the cheek, I floated up the stairs and into bed. I was out like a light.

Chapter 11: Carabalk Isle

    Waking up early, I showered and race downstairs for breakfast. It was going to be a great day. I could feel it. Today was the day we were going to be the day we get Daniel back.
    My father and mother were already eating breakfast when I got into the kitchen.
    "Because today is going to be a big day, I cooked you a full Irish, Jackie," My dad said as I sat down. Two rashers (bacon for the Americans), two sausages, two hash browns, two eggs, two white pudding and two black puddings, beans, tea and toast.

Irish Spy Agency (ISA) Chronicles Book 2: Chain Retrieval

The perfect Irish breakfast for anyone visiting Ireland. "There is more in the oven." "Thanks Dad," I began, "I'm going to need the extra fuel today. I have a feeling things are going to be great."

I was just finishing up when my watched beep. *"Jackie, can you come in now before everyone else does please."* "I'll be there in five Paul."

I washed up the dishes before I said goodbye to my parents and headed out the back door.

Stepping outside my watch beep and my jetpack appeared on my back.

I flew straight to vinegar Hill and into Paul's lair. As I walked into the main room, Paul was not the only one there. David was there too with a few other ISA staff I assumed.

"Hey Paul," I said as they were all talking and never noticed my entrance, "Why did I need to come in early?"

"Oh Jackie," Paul began, "David and the ISA, want to know your plan on getting Daniel back." I glanced around at all of them and noticed David smirking.

"I have no plan," I lied, "All my plans come to me in the moment they are needed remember."

"Jackie," David spoke, "I can't have someone like that as a leader of a team. My team leaders need to be able to make plans in advance and let their team know before the head into battle."

"I'm sorry to hear that David," I stated, "But you're not my boss and you're not Paul's boss. So I will lead my team my way. That is why I was chosen by team as the leader. If you want to report to the real boss, there's the door. Don't let it hit you on the way out."

"Jackie," Paul shouted, "You cannot talk to your superiors like that." "Paul, I know you are friends with David here but I can't change my way of being just because he is worried about his son."

Everyone was quiet for a moment. "David I'm sorry you are missing your son and I promise you my team and I will bring Daniel home and we won't stop at anything to make it happen."

"Jackie, I appreciate your honesty," David said, "Unlike Paul, I don't mind when inferior speaks to superiors like that. Makes me proud to know that ISA agents will stand up for themselves regardless of the person and their role."

David and the ISA associates left after that. "Paul, I'm sorry," I began, "You will understand soon enough why I was so ignorant, I promise you that it will be all worthwhile."

Just as I said that, my team walked in. "Someone having secret meetings without their team?" Rachel questioned.

"Everything is all good," I answered, "Some ISA agents came to chat to me." I noticed Alice staring at me, knowing that she knows exactly what is happening but understand where I am coming from.

Irish Spy Agency (ISA) Chronicles Book 2: Chain Retrieval

"Paul found Carabalk Isle," Alice stated changing the subject.

"Paul," I said shockingly, "You never said."

"Sorry I was going to tell you before the team got here when the ISA officials left."

"Yes I found Carabalk Isle and it's a lot closer than we think."

"What do you mean by that Paul?" Molly asked, "I'm guessing we are below it. Am I right?"

"You are right Molly," Paul said, "If you go now you will get there but it changes places again."

We all ran out the door and into the sky. Flying straight up into the sky.

"Molly show us the way," I told her as I flew beside her. Molly closed her eyes as we flew up further and further.

She stop flying and was just floating there so we all starting floating beside her. Looking in the direction Molly was staring . We followed her eyes.

Carabalk Isle was beautiful. We flew straight into the middle of the Isle.

This place was the most beautiful place I've ever seen. I could see they were so many animals here that were considered extinct.

Sabor-Tooth Tigers were here, Woolly Mammoths, Dire Wolves, woolly rhino's and there was so many more here. They all gathered round us as we landed.

"Molly, do you sense where you chain is?" Alice and I asked at the same time.

Molly closed her eyes as the rest of looked around the Isle. "Molly," Denny spoke up, "I think I found your chain."

We all looked over where Denny was pointed. Something was shimmering on one of the sabor-tooth tiger neck. It had to be around the most dangerous animal up here.

"Molly," I said, "You really want to go get that"
"Of course I do," She confidently said, "With Jaden's help of course."

I glanced at Jaden who was looking very nervous. "Jaden, you don't have too," I announced.

"Yes I do," He answered, "I have to do this for the team."

"The rest of us can protect against any threats," I announced. Molly and Jaden walked closer to the sabor-tooth tiger as the rest of us circle them in, "Alice you should help them, just in case," I said as I glanced at her.

The rest of us focus on the surroundings but I was trying to focus on both so no one would get hurt.

Jaden slowly approached the sabor-tooth tiger even though the tiger was growling at him. *"I'm not going to hurt you. It's ok I promise."* Jaden kept saying as he slowly approached.

He was about ten feet away when the sabor-tooth tiger leaped onto Jaden growling and slobbering all over him.

Irish Spy Agency (ISA) Chronicles Book 2: Chain Retrieval

Jaden was so quiet underneath the tiger which was shocking and confusing. I did remember that Jaden's power could have been something to do with animals.

I had no need to worry about them. The sabor-tooth tiger stop growling and laid down beside Jaden as he was rubbing the large cat's chest.

"Molly," Jaden started, "Come here slowly, calm your breathing. Let the cat know you are no threat."

Molly slowly walked over to Jaden and laid on the ground beside them. As she rubbed the cat's neck and chest, she slowly took the chain off.

Jaden stayed down and played with the cat as Molly slowed stepped away. "Alice, time to make the kitty go away," I said, "Make a giant laser and send him into the forest. We have incoming."

Everyone looked up. Daniel and a whole heap of goons were coming for us.

"Time to kick our plan into action," I said as everyone nodded and got into place as Molly placed the chain around her neck.

All the animals disappeared as we were surrounded by Daniel and the goons. To kick the plan into action we needed to get Daniel in between us.

"Now Alice," I screamed. She pointed at Daniel and swung her arm around behind us as Daniel gave flying over us. "Let's do this."

Irish Spy Agency (ISA) Chronicles Book 2: Chain Retrieval

Everyone got into their position as the plan began. Daniel was struggling to move behind us. The plan was working.

"You all go help the others," Nick screamed, "Protect them as I fight these goons, if any slip by, you get them." We surrounded the others Nick duplicated himself.

Alice had Daniel wriggling on the ground trying to escape, "Now guys," I said to Jaden, Mike, Rachel, and Denny.

As the stood for the map that time to activate it, Mike had two fingers pointed at Daniel as a mini tornado headed towards Daniel.

Jaden had his hand in a claw and sent brick, mud and stone towards Daniel. Denny had made a fist and hit Daniel with fire.

Rachel hands was kind of weird, but sent a waterfall of sorts at the Daniel. Her index and middle finger made a 'v' pointing up, another 'v' at the side and her thumbs was the side.

I could see Daniel struggling to get away from everyone but when I glanced at Alice she wasn't even breaking a sweat.

This plan was working. When I looked around at Nick he was doing great keeping the goons off us and getting to Daniel. This was happening for so long we forgot where we were.

"We have to get off this Isle," I announced, "Unfortunately we've been destroying the place.

Irish Spy Agency (ISA) Chronicles Book 2: Chain Retrieval

The animals will come and get us of the island themselves."

We all were looking around and the tree were rustling. We turn our focus back on Daniel and I could see something happening to him.

"Bring him home guys," I spoke to Denny, Jaden, Mike, and Rachel, "It's time to finish this up so we can leave."

They forced more power out towards Daniel who was completely covered with all the powers like in a cocoon.

As we focus on Daniel we never noticed one of the goons get passed Nick and he attacked Alice. Knocking her flying and losing control on Daniel.

The gang still focused their power on Daniel but Daniel wasn't having any of it. He sent a shockwave toward us as he burst out of the cocoon and sent us flying backward.

I was the first to my feet, Daniel was still floating in the air covered in white light. As he slowly floated to the ground, I got into my fighting stance not sure if everything worked.

Daniel looked at me when he landed, "Jackie, I have so much to tell you," he announced.

I hugged Daniel so happy the plan worked. "Daniel, help get our team and when we get back to Paul's lair we can chat."

"Already done," Daniel said, " The power of duplication comes in handy, "I've also healed them so we can leave."

Irish Spy Agency (ISA) Chronicles Book 2: Chain Retrieval

As we all gather round each other to leave, the goons started to attacked us. "We can do this," I shouted, "Let's protect each other, the Isle and all the creatures on it."

All ten of us back together, this was going to epic. The goons attacked us from all around us so we went back to back. Five on either side.

Just as we were going to attack, the animals came out of the forest and attacked the goons with us. "Jaden and Daniel go protect the animals, the rest of us got the goons."

Daniel picked Jaden up and flew towards the animals. As they protected and fought alongside the animals, the rest of us attacked the goons from our side.

As we fought hand to hand and power to power, I knew we had to get out of here soon so the animals could be safe from everyone again.

'Alice and Daniel, we need to get all the goons out of here so we can fix this place up and leave and never come back.'

I love communicating mentally with Alice and Daniel because it protects everyone. *'Let's do it Daniel.'*

Alice and Daniel both flew up into the air. We couldn't see what was happening but suddenly the goons were gone and we were alone.

Alice and Daniel came back and landed in front of me. "We did it y'all. Group hug."

Irish Spy Agency (ISA) Chronicles Book 2: Chain Retrieval

As we hugged, I noticed Daniel was about to say something, "Let's clean up here and put everything back to where it is supposed to."

"We got this guys," Jaden said, "Nick, Jackie, Molly, and Peter, you guys just relax. The rest of us let's get to work."

"Except you Denny," I jumped in the air, "We don't need anything burning down while we are here."

Denny sat down beside the rest of us. "Sorry for jumping in there Daniel," I said as we waited, "I know you have many things to say."

"I just want to apologize for everything," he stated. "There is nothing to apologize for Daniel," Alice announced, "You were not you when did all those things."

We sat there in silence watching everything around us as the gang finished.

The creatures came over to us as the gang landed back beside us. "We are so sorry to have brought the goons here and destroyed everything," Jaden said rubbing the sabor-tooth tiger that had Molly's chain on.

The tiger growled at Jaden, "We will be back when the case is finished to hang out. I promise," Jaden said as the tiger brushed against his new friend.

"Let's get out here guys," I announced as the portal opened. We all stepped through the portal and into Paul's lair.

Irish Spy Agency (ISA) Chronicles Book 2: Chain Retrieval

Paul was just finishing up a zoom call as we walked in. "Paul," I announced, "We have completed this part of the mission. Daniel is back with us."

"Oh Daniel," Paul exclaimed, "Your parents are going to be over the moon you are back."

"About that actually," Daniel began, "That is one of things I want to talked to you all about."

"You can tell us anything," Alice stated, "We are not going to judge you."

"Well, while I was on the other team, I finally figure out who is behind these goons. And I know some of their plan."

"Firstly," Paul said, "Tell us who the leader is, that is the most important part at the moment."

"You guys won't believe me when I tell," He stated, "I'm still shocked myself but the leader of the goons is...."

To Be Continued.

Check out The beginning of The Irish Spy Agency (ISA) Chronicles in the first book Available on Amazon as well.

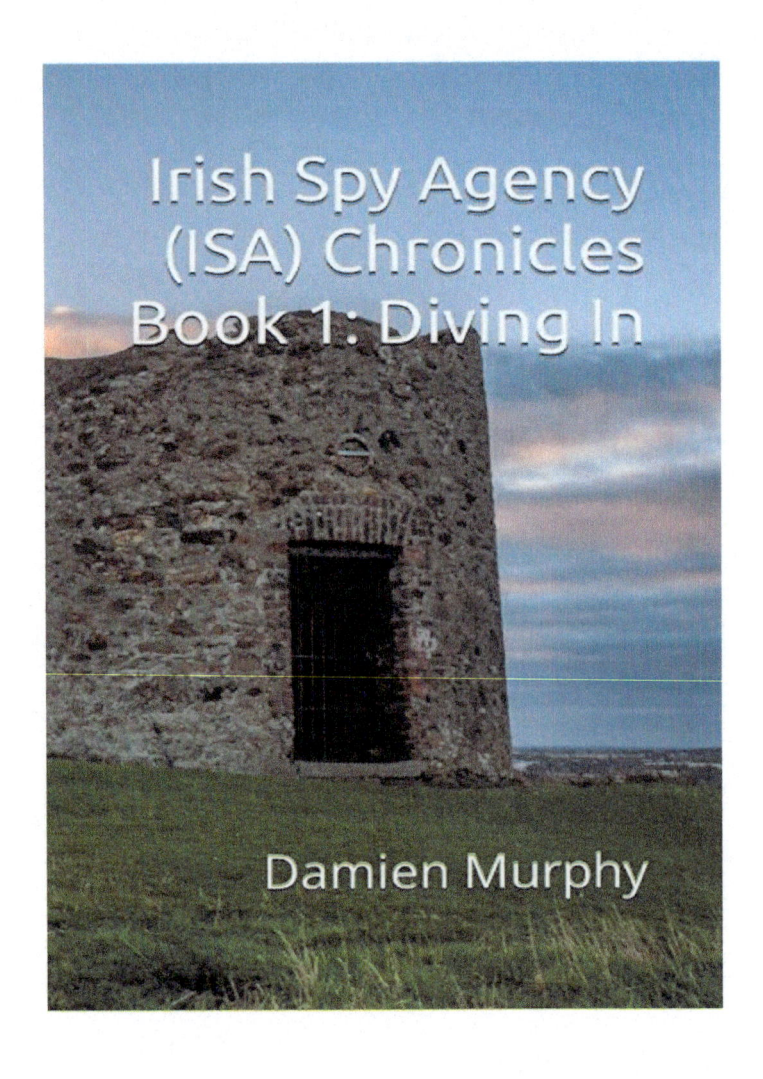

Irish Spy Agency (ISA) Chronicles Book 1: Diving In

Damien Murphy

About The Author

Living in Enniscorthy, Co Wexford my entire life so far, I have visited very few places in the world. One of the places I have visited is Jacob's Ladder in Abilene Texas at Abilene Christian Union which is part of this book and on the cover.

I have also loved reading my entire life. I will read any type of fiction but my favourite are books on the supernatural side of things: Vampires, Werewolves and Witches Like Twilight and The Vampire Diaries but I also love books on Dystopian Worlds like The Hunger games and The Divergent Series.

My English Teacher Ms Jessica Doyle and the School Librarian Ms. Éadaoin Quinn are the people to thank for my love of writing as I spent my five years in Enniscorthy Community College as it is called now falling in love with writing. In those five years Ms Doyle and Ms Quinn both help me and hone my writing skills. So a big shout out to Ms Jessica Doyle and Ms Éadaoin Quinn.

Printed in Great Britain
by Amazon